This time, he did smile, and it was quite a show. She nearly felt her knees weaken, which was ridiculous. This kind of thing didn't happen. Love at first sight wasn't real.

He scratched his temple. "I'm fine. Been through a lot worse than a duffel bag hitting me over the head followed by a beautiful bride jumping my bones."

"My bag *hit* you? Oh, I'm so sorry. Again." She held out her hand while looking up at the balcony. Still no sign of Ivan but he could find her at any moment. "I'm Phoebe."

"Wherever you're going, need a ride?" His curious eyes, missing nothing, followed her gaze to the third-floor balcony and then back to her. "Is there a church somewhere, missing a bride?"

WELCOME TO MIRACLE BAY!

THE TROUBLE WITH A KISS

A SUNSET KISS NOVEL

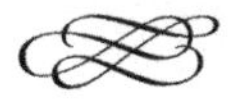

HEATHERLY BELL

For my mother, who believes in miracles and taught me everything I know.

CHAPTER 1

"True love is like ghosts. Something everyone talks about, but few have ever seen."
~ François de La Rochefoucauld

When the sedan approached the curb, the Uber driver cocked his head, probably doubting he was in the right place. Or whether maybe someone had played a prank on him.

Because Phoebe Carrington wore a wedding dress.

The moment he stopped, she ran to the car, hauled open the passenger door, and threw in her duffel bag.

"Hello, sir. Yes, I called for a ride. It was me. Thank you for coming."

Phoebe struggled to climb inside the back seat of the car while wearing several yards of satin, tulle, and lace. Difficult, as this dress had its own zip code. First, she tried to get one leg in, then the other. Going in butt first didn't work because then half the gown was riding outside. Pretty soon she wouldn't care what happened to this ridiculous dress that hadn't been her choice anyway. Aunt Sarah thought it would make Phoebe look like a princess.

Finally, Phoebe gathered the long train and shoved the yards of material in first, then sat on it. She managed to buckle, even though she sat about a foot higher than normal. The top of her head and tiara grazed the ceiling of the car.

"How does this work? Do I pay you now or later? I'm an Uber-virgin. I downloaded the app a few minutes ago."

"Ah...well..." the man said, staring at her through the rearview mirror. All Phoebe could see were two bushy eyebrows meeting his forehead.

This was what happened when a reluctant bride left her sedan at her father's home and took a limousine to the wedding. No car available for a clean getaway.

The driver remained speechless, then he looked across the street at the church. He glanced back at Phoebe and quirked a brow.

"We'll worry about how I pay you later," Phoebe said with a dismissive wave. "Can we drive now, please? I'm kind of in a hurry. Go!"

He pulled out into the bustle of traffic. "You entered that you wanted to go to the airport? Is that still...right?"

"No, actually, the airport was a placeholder. I had to put something in, didn't I? Can you take me to a hotel, maybe on the other side of the city? Someplace reasonable, not expensive."

Phoebe had to change out of her wedding dress first, then she'd make a plan. The airport was a possibility, but at the moment she needed to be away from the church where by now they'd probably started to play the "Wedding March." And Aunt Sarah, who'd given Phoebe a wide opening when she left to check on the bridesmaids, would soon realize she was missing a bride.

Traffic as they weaved through San Francisco was a snarl, but her driver seemed an expert. He bounced in and out of lanes, making Phoebe feel like a criminal on the run. The label fit in some ways. She clutched the grab handle and watched as the traffic parted for her crazy driver.

This hadn't been the plan.

In another reality, she would be walking down the aisle, to assure Ethan Bellamy that she would love, honor, and cherish him for as long as they both shall live.

Phoebe had planned to say, "I do," but somehow her feet grew a mind of their own. They said, "I don't" and flew out the doors of the church when Aunt Sarah wasn't looking.

A few minutes later, the driver pulled over to a modest-looking hotel and went around to help Phoebe out of the back seat.

"Miss, are you going to be okay?"

"Yes, thank you so much."

Phoebe was not at all sure that she'd ever be okay again, but that wasn't this poor man's concern. He'd done his job, so she added a hefty tip and sent him on his way.

Sure, she drew a few questioning looks when she walked through the double doors of the hotel and up to the check-in desk. But, hey, this was San Francisco after all, and stranger things had happened.

In fact, the desk clerk didn't blink an eye. "Can I help you?"

"I'd like a room for the night, please."

"Just one night?"

"Yes, I…I think so." All she had to do was change out of her dress and figure out her next moves.

"I'll need a credit card."

Phoebe fished in her bag. A few minutes later, she was in a modest third-floor room with a balcony and a street view. One full-size bed, a couple of nightstands on either side. A desk. A little coffee machine on the dresser. A clean bathroom. Nothing fancy, which suited her fine. Maybe Phoebe could stay here for a while.

Or she should just head to the airport and buy a ticket to New York.

She couldn't face anyone right now, least of all her father. Her cell had blown up with text messages and missed calls. But Phoebe couldn't bring herself to look. Her father would be concerned, her groom furious.

Who would dare to stand up Ethan Bellamy, the Silicon Valley CEO worth billions?

Phoebe would.

Eventually, she would face everyone. Aunt Sarah, who had largely planned the wedding. Her father, who'd wanted this marriage. Ethan, who didn't love her, but wanted to marry her for some odd reason. She imagined he viewed her as his latest investment. Marry the daughter of one of his toughest competitors and maybe those pesky monopoly lawsuits would go away. And Phoebe had wanted to please her father, but it turned out the price of her heart and soul were too high.

Glancing at the digital clock on the nightstand she noted that, by now, her father might be scouring the church, Ethan sending his bodyguards and business associates to search the building. Maybe they'd even be worried about her.

Phoebe needed help, posthaste, but everyone in the world who loved and supposedly cared for her was inside a church. They all expected her to go through with this sham marriage, this wedding to a man thirty years her senior. To be fair, Phoebe had *told* them she would. And she'd fully expected to, for months, until she peeked inside the church and witnessed her future.

The Silicon Valley elite, dozens of her father's friends and associates lined the pews. Many of her Stanford classmates, too, those who'd alternatively made her life miserable and at other times been the only friends she had.

Ethan, her husband to be, fifty-nine years old to her twenty-nine, stood arrogantly at the altar in his black designer tux. Self-assured. Confident. Why not? He got everything he wanted the moment he wanted it, and now sat at the helm of a former start-up which held a monopoly over the software industry.

Phoebe loved her father, and because he'd suggested this arrangement would be in her best interest, she'd gone along with the idea. As she had with anything he'd asked of her nearly every day of her twenty-nine years. She did as she was told, grateful because with her mother gone, Daddy and Aunt Sarah, his only sibling, were all she had left in the world by way of family. They both expected her gratitude. Having attended the best schools in the country and grown up with every privilege, it would be a sin for Phoebe not to be grateful, happy, and self-fulfilled.

And after twenty-nine saintly years, she'd just become a sinner in the worst way. She'd finally reached the point at which she could no longer cede control over her life and go along to make peace. Not with something this important.

Her gaze flashed around the average furnishings of the room, panic spreading like celebrity gossip. Palms sweaty? Check. Heart racing? Yes, sir. She'd never done anything this rash in her life.

No one should find her in this modest hotel, and given traffic, she figured she had *at least* a few more minutes. Maybe longer. They'd have to find her first, then drive here. And unless they drove kamikaze style like her Uber guy, it might take a while. Surely by tonight she'd have a plan. One option was to buy a plane ticket to New York City. Start over.

One of her old friends and Stanford classmates had relocated there a few years ago and started a small publishing press. Phoebe's resources were few, but she had the credit card that she'd used to book the room. Her only clothes were in the duffel she'd brought to church, where she'd changed. Inside were the slacks she'd worn, blouse, flats, wallet, makeup, and a few odds and ends. Nothing to sustain her for a long getaway.

Not an auspicious beginning.

Coward. I'm a coward. I have to face Daddy. Face them all.

Oh God, oh God, oh God. What have I done?

Unable to resist any longer, Phoebe picked up her phone and checked her text messages. Ethan had texted he was worried about her. Where was she? Could he send a car for her? She was late and people were beginning to talk.

Not: honey, tell me where you are, and I'll come get you. We can work this out, whatever it is. I'm nervous, too.

Those would be the words of a man who adored his bride. But they didn't have that kind of relationship, or barely one at all. Ethan's words were those of a CEO who wasn't used to waiting for *anyone.*

Phoebe had to explain what she'd done to at least one person. This way they would know she didn't need any help.

She dialed Flannery, her cousin and maid of honor.

Flannery sounded breathless when she picked up. "Where are you? Everyone is frantic."

"I'm okay. P-please tell everyone not to worry about me."

"Not to *worry* about you? You're supposed to be getting married right now!"

"I know, but...I'm not coming."

"You're not...you're not *coming*?" Flannery whispered. "But Ethan..."

"He doesn't love me. And I don't love him."

"It doesn't matter whether he loves you or not. Just marry him, and live separate lives. That's what we do."

But Phoebe's late mother, Becky, had loved her husband. She wouldn't have married someone she *didn't* love. Her mother's memory even now gave Phoebe strength.

"I should have never agreed to marry him. You know me. I didn't have the guts to stand my ground."

"And now? Why now? Phoebe, you're going to humiliate him...he won't take this well."

"I'm sorry. Really sorry. Tell Ethan I'll get in touch with him later. But don't come looking for me. I need a little time."

"Where are you?"

"The airport," Phoebe lied.

"That's strange. Your Find My Friends location shows you're on Mission Street. What are you doing there?"

"If you knew, why did you ask? Promise you won't tell anyone! Look, I'll call you back."

"But—"

Phoebe threw her phone on the bed and sat for several more minutes. She *should* face her father and Ethan. Tell them she was worth more, she deserved more, she wanted more from a husband. She *demanded* more. True love, for instance. Affection and tenderness.

Phoebe strode into the bathroom and took a good look at herself in the mirror. Dear God, she still wore her tiara. Styled over a chignon that the hairstylist hired by Aunt Sarah had suggested, it felt glued to her cranium. Phoebe, who usually wore her dark hair down, didn't even look like herself. The woman that stared back at her was a phony. An impostor. The real Phoebe Carrington had a lot more hutzpah than someone who would run out of the church without facing everyone.

You are going to do great things with your life.

The mantra, the affirmation that her mother had recited to her every night before bedtime came back. It was time for Phoebe to remember. To recite it to herself. And she would add one:

You are going to find true love.

It exists.

Twisting off the three-carat diamond ring, she gently laid it on the bed.

Ethan had given her the ring between phone calls over dinner. He thought she'd sucked in a breath at the beauty of the gem and smiled with smug satisfaction. But she'd been utterly disgusted by the size of the rock. It could probably feed a small nation, and she was to wear it on her finger…for the rest of her *life.*

But she hadn't said a word as she accepted it, reminding herself of all the charities that Ethan funded. Maybe she should take this ring with her now, sell it, and do some good. But it wasn't hers. Not anymore. She was done being the sacrificial lamb.

The show was over.

"Phoebe! Phoebe Carrington!" A man's voice boomed from the hallway.

Oh no. How had they…? Had Flannery said something? It couldn't have been *her.* There hadn't been enough time since their conversation. Unless…

Her phone, the damn tracking device! *The leash!* Years ago, she'd shared her Find Your Friends location with her father. Every now and then he'd text and ask whether or not she'd had a good day. He'd gently chide her for still being at work even if he'd been the one to teach her a strong work ethic. She'd thought it sweet and not at all an invasion of her privacy.

"Phoebe? We know you're here! Come on out. I'm not leaving until you do."

She recognized the voice and opened the door to peek down the hall. It wasn't her father, or Ethan. This was Ethan's bodyguard, Ivan, the Russian who reminded her of a mobster.

He banged on the door of a room four down from hers. "Is Phoebe Carrington here?"

"Do I *look* like a *Phoebe Carrington*?" A woman answered. "And who the hell is Phoebe Carrington?"

"She's late for a wedding," he shouted.

Oh, hell no. It will not go down this way.

She'd come too far, and she wasn't going to walk out of this hotel room and surrender. Let him pry off the doors of every single room, with a court order of some kind. She wished him luck. Phoebe grabbed her bag, leaving her phone next to the ring. They'd find both eventually, but they wouldn't find *her*.

That's it. No more Miss Nice Gal. Uh-uh. She'd go out the back rather than hide in this room like a mouse. No time to change out of her wedding dress now. Opening the sliders, she stepped onto the balcony and peeked at the street view below. A fire escape led all the way to the ground floor, where she'd make a run for it. She threw her bag down first, then put one heeled pump on the rung. Unfortunately, it wasn't easy to go down a ladder wearing a wedding dress and heels. Turned out to be much tougher than getting in a car.

She held up her dress, the train tripping her a couple of times. Eventually she made it down the ladder to the second floor. By the next ladder, she'd gotten the hang of it, gathering the yards of material in one hand. She made it to the first floor. Almost free! But something happened on the way to the ground floor. The fire escape gave way, and Phoebe grabbed on to the rail, hanging from it like a desperate monkey.

She heard cursing from below and saw a man rubbing his head. Her duffel bag lay at his feet.

"What the...?" the man said as he caught sight of her swinging above him.

"I'm so sorry, sir," she managed between huffs and puffs of the important work of breathing. "Would you mind helping me out, please? Could you put that ladder back where it belongs?"

"You're only ten feet from the ground floor if that. Just jump and I'll catch you."

Great, she'd run into a comedian.

"Thank you so much, sir, but I don't want to impose. If you could just put the ladder back and be on your way I would...be...ever so grateful."

"Sorry, lady, that ladder isn't going back. It's broken."

Oh, fudge on a stick, just her luck. "Could you...would you mind driving your car over as close as you can and then I could fall on the roof?"

This seemed like her best idea.

"Well, first, my truck is a few blocks from here. Do we have that kind of time?" His voice had taken on a "poor me, dealing with the crazy lady" tone.

"But I...I don't think I can jump."

"Sure, you can. I figure that dress is going to work a bit like a parachute. Slow you down and cushion your fall. And you're not jumping, you're dropping. It's really not that far. I'll help. I do this for a living."

Really. He walked around the city cushioning the falls of runaway brides as they clung from broken fire escapes. She wanted to bite back with a smart aleck remark, but right now he was her only friend. Passersby were beginning to stare. She must cut quite the sight, wearing a wedding dress, dangling helplessly. Sooner or later, Ivan would knock on every single door and it would become a simple process of elimination. And what would happen if he heard a commotion outside? Sirens? Horns? Cheering from a small crowd?

Jump! Jump! Jump!

"I could call the fire department. I'm off duty, but we can get the ladder truck over here in a few minutes. It seems like a waste of taxpayer dollars, if I'm being honest. I'm already here."

"Well, that's okay, I don't want to bother the fire department."

But her hands were beginning to ache from the effort of holding up the weight of her body. This dress gave her at least an extra five pounds of material.

She swung her legs, catching nothing but air.

If it were possible, she could almost *hear* him roll his eyes. "Look, I'll count you down. I'll count to three, then you jump, and I'll be ready. You look light enough. I've got you."

Phoebe didn't know whether this had anything to do with the last moments before she plunged to her death, but this man's voice had a certain warm quality to it. Like her favorite snack as a child: cinnamon sugar on hot buttered toast. He sounded like melted cocoa. Assurance and confidence poured from every word he said. Not arrogance, no. Just certainty.

At this point she had little choice. "But why on the count of three? Why not five? Or ten? Then I can prepare myself."

"One," he said with authority.

"Really, I don't want to bother you…it was simply a question."

"Two."

"There has to be a better way."

But her choices had led her to this moment and now she had to make a decision. Let Ivan find her, if she lived that long, or take a real risk and jump to a new life.

Oh, excuse her, *drop* to her new life.

Literally.

"Thr—"

Phoebe Carrington let go of the little certainty she had left in her world and plunged.

CHAPTER 2

"When I saw you, I fell I love. And you smiled,
because you knew." ~
William Shakespeare

"Oooph."

The train of her dress ripped, and Phoebe nearly flattened the man who had promised to catch her.

"You weren't supposed to go *on* three," he grumbled from under her, thankfully still among the living. "I said *after* three."

Phoebe pushed up with her elbows, taking her weight off him. She was sprawled on top of him, legs across his hips in an indecent position.

"I'm sorry, sorry, I'm so sorry, um...sir."

She hesitated before *sir* because this close up, hands clasped to his shoulders, she clearly saw this man was about *her* age. And pretty damn swoony. While swinging from a fire escape pondering imminent death, this was not any of her concern, but now that she wasn't going to die, she noticed.

"Don't call me *sir.*"

The man had wavy dark hair, and a strong chiseled jaw covered with a light scruff of beard. His intense eyes were an interesting brown, a shade between caramel and whiskey. Sensual lips tipped up on one corner of a bemused half smile.

Oh yeah. She was still straddling him.

A sharp sting of awareness slammed into her and the air around them glowed in a golden hue. Prickles of desire sliced through her body, the blood rushing too fast to her head. She was at once hot and shivering. What was wrong with her? Had the fall done some damage to her brain? A concussion? Was she having a stroke? But no, she saw *him* clearly, his intelligent eyes curious and questioning. The colors around him shimmered, clear and bright. She shook her head and blinked a few times.

"Do you mind?" he asked, rubbing his head.

She climbed off and stood, shaking off the crazy sensations and visions, and searching for her bag. It was nearby, so she picked it up and gave him one last longing look. What a terrible time to meet a man like him. Too bad she was on her way to a new life.

"Thank you for saving me."

He stood and brushed himself off. "I didn't *save* you, but you're welcome. I'm Marco Reyes. Can I get you to a hospital...or something?"

"No, I'm fine. No injuries. At least, I don't think so. But are *you* okay? I nearly squashed you. Can I pay for your medical bills? I have a credit card." She reached into the bag for her wallet. The card was another good way for her father to track her, since their accounts were linked. "I probably can't use it anymore, so you may as well take it."

This time, he did smile, and it was quite a show. She

nearly felt her knees weaken, which was ridiculous. This kind of thing didn't happen. Love at first sight wasn't real.

He scratched his temple. "I'm fine. Been through a lot worse than a duffel bag hitting me over the head followed by a beautiful bride jumping my bones."

"My bag *hit* you? Oh, I'm so sorry. Again." She held out her hand while looking up at the balcony. Still no sign of Ivan but he could find her at any moment. "I'm Phoebe."

"Wherever you're going, need a ride?" His curious eyes, missing nothing, followed her gaze to the third-floor balcony and then back to her. "Is there a church somewhere, missing a bride?"

As if assessing her condition, and her state of dress, his gaze slid up and down her body a few times. There was nothing wolfish or leering about it. And she felt safe with this man, though she didn't quite understand why. By now, she should have learned the hard way not to trust anyone.

She caught him staring at the top of her head and it wasn't until then she realized she hadn't removed the tiara.

Self-consciously her hand rose to adjust it and clutched her duffel to her chest. "I-I don't know where I'm going."

"That sure makes it easier for me."

This man obviously wanted to help her, but Phoebe didn't want him caught up in her drama. She'd already hurt him enough. She looked up at the balcony above her, trying to think where she'd go from here. Another hotel room in the city? Without her phone, no one could track her. What would someone else do in this situation? Someone who wasn't Phoebe Carrington?

"Well…if you insist, I would appreciate a ride. I don't want him to find me."

His smile evaporated. "Let's get going."

. . .

MARCO KEPT his hand low on Phoebe's back, guiding her quickly and efficiently to his truck. He checked behind him every few seconds to make certain they weren't being followed.

Of all the things he'd planned for tonight, helping a princess bride escape from her third-floor balcony was not on the list. The guys at the station would have a blast with this one. He was often called the "black cloud" because action happened within minutes of him showing up on the job, but this was a first.

With the next two days off, he had plans for some downtime. He'd been headed to Juan's Bar and Grill for some Mexican food and a game of pool with the Firehouse 54 crew. His older brother, Dylan, and Dylan's fiancée, Charley, were already there.

But despite his plans, Marco was not one to turn down a woman in need. He'd call this his good deed for the day. Father Suarez had encouraged him to stop worrying about proving himself on the job and instead focus on how he could help others. Opportunities to help people were everywhere. But Marco was pretty sure Father Suarez wasn't talking *literal* rescues.

Especially not of runaway brides.

Marco opened the passenger side door of his truck, holding it for Phoebe. He took one look at her dress and for the second time tonight was stumped.

"That's…a lot of dress."

"Tell me about it. At least you have a big truck. I made it into a sedan in this dress, so I think this should be a lot easier."

But it wasn't simple for her to climb inside the truck with several feet of fluffy material in her way. She pushed the dress in first and climbed in, surrounded by a cloud of white on either side. Like a human Q-tip.

"I'm fine." She nodded.

Not at all sure of that, he shoved more of the dress inside and managed to shut the door.

Okay. So, *this* was happening.

Marco pulled out onto the street, glimpsing in his rearview mirror. A large man ran toward them, dressed in a black suit.

He waved and screamed, "Phoebe! Come back!"

"Go, go!" Phoebe urged, hand on Marco's arm. "Faster!"

He obliged, peeling ahead of traffic and earning a few honks.

"Okay." He relaxed once they were a few blocks away. "Want to tell me what's going on?"

"Not really," she said. "Is that okay?"

"I guess it's not any of my business, but that man seemed pretty upset." He eyed her extremely white dress. "And you were obviously on your way to a special event."

He wondered how anyone got all the way to the altar and changed their mind. Surely there would have been warning signs before the moment. Some red flags. Long ago he'd decided he'd marry only once, if that, but if he ever felt this kind of pressure of making a mistake, he might just slip out the back, too.

Or down the fire escape.

"Can we just say I changed my mind?"

"Was that your groom back there?" He didn't think chasing down one's bride was the best way to start a marriage, but what did he know. "Is this something that can be fixed? Maybe if you talked it over?"

"No, it *can't* be fixed."

"Look, princess, you won't get any judgment from me. I don't understand how two people can agree to love and honor each other for the rest of their lives. It's too big of a commitment to wrap my head around."

"That's part of it. I knew this was wrong from the beginning, but my fiancé was very persuasive."

"Guess marriage isn't for everyone."

"Oh, I believe in marriage, but it has to be with the right person. It has to be because you love each other so much that you can't stand the idea of being apart."

"Why *else* would anyone get married?"

"Sometimes…there are reasons."

"Like being pregnant?"

"Oh my God, no. I'm not *pregnant*!"

"I didn't say you were. Maybe that's a good reason to get married, I don't know. Beyond that, I'm stumped."

"It seemed like a good idea at the time."

Marco snorted. "You must be compatible."

"No…not really."

"I guess opposites attract."

"Not in my case."

Wow. Okay. He was zero for two. And in his truck with a possibly unstable runaway bride, going nowhere fast. Surprisingly, it wasn't unpleasant.

Marco liked women, but from the moment she'd fallen on him, he'd experienced a different kind of awareness. An immediate pull and attraction. An almost electrical sensation coursed through him, one he felt to the soles of his feet. If he believed in love at first sight, which he *didn't*, he'd imagine it went something like this. Even if he'd literally been hit over the head, what had come later was more of a buzzing sensation. Pleasant. A glow. He'd stayed on the ground simply stunned, triaging himself for a mild concussion.

When she'd straddled him in her big poufy dress, his mind had gone places it had no business going. But she had smooth creamy skin and bright eyes framed by thick lashes. Brown hair in a bun, she wore a crown.

A *crown.*

"Well, how about it? Where should I take you? What about your family? You said you didn't know where you were going. Family is a good place to start."

"I can't see my family right now. My father will be very upset with me."

"Right. All that money. I know weddings aren't cheap."

Charley and Dylan were making plans and looking at venues. He'd almost had a cardiac event when he'd seen the prices of some of those places. Marriage was expensive and it was a good thing for him he couldn't afford it.

When she didn't answer, but continued to gnaw on her lower lip, he offered what he thought she might actually need. "How about a shelter? There's one not far from here."

"You mean like for the homeless? That should be for people who really *need* the help."

"I was thinking of a women's shelter." Marco spoke carefully. "For women who want help getting out of abusive relationships."

"Oh, no, that's not me!"

Of course, she would say that. "That man looked pretty angry back there."

"He wouldn't hurt me."

"Whatever you say, but being left at the altar might make a man pretty desperate."

"Oh, that wasn't my *groom*."

Right.

"Well, I think I better mind my own business from this point. Where can I take you?"

"I don't want to put you out any more than I already have," she said. "Why don't you just take me along, wherever you were going? I'll figure it out from there."

"I was meeting my brother and the rest of the crew for some dinner and pool."

"Well, I don't have a swimsuit, but I could watch you guys swim."

"Huh?" He blinked. She was a strange one. "Listen, you worry me."

"Please don't. I'll be fine."

Marco wasn't so sure. "When you apparently have no place to stay?"

"Maybe there's a cheap hotel around here somewhere. Mostly, I just need to change into regular clothes. I'll figure it all out then."

"I don't want to take you to any ratty old hotel. That could be dangerous for other reasons."

"Right now, I need somewhere I can get out of this dress."

"If that's all, I can take you to my place to change."

"Do you live around here?"

"The marina."

"I would appreciate that. After that, I'll be on my way and won't bother you anymore."

A few minutes later, Marco pulled into the marina. He rented an old and retired fishing boat. It made for a nomadic kind of lifestyle, but it suited him.

"You live on a houseboat?"

"I live on a boat. Not exactly a houseboat. I'm between places and it's cheap rent in the city."

"Wow. So cool." She unstrapped her seat belt.

"I sure hope it can accommodate your dress."

He went around and gave her a hand, but when she struggled again, caught between the skirt of the dress and that long trailing part, he took matters into his own hands.

Hands on either side of her waist, he pulled. And heard another loud rip.

He winced. "I hope you don't care about this dress."

She eyed what was left of it. Several feet, by his estimation.

"It wasn't even my choice, to be honest."

Marco didn't even know how to respond to that.

"This way, princess." He waved a hand in the direction of his boat slip.

He couldn't imagine what kind of a picture they made. She was suddenly walking strangely, dragging one leg. The dress probably made it difficult to walk but he hoped she hadn't been injured on top of everything else. If so, he'd have to take her to the ER to get checked out and he'd wind up spending a lot more time with this bridal accident waiting to happen.

Making himself useful, he stopped to gather the ripped part of the dress that dragged behind her. He held it off the ground so she could walk easier, and he followed. What was the name of the person who walked behind the bride up the aisle, carrying the train of the dress?

Groomsman?

Ringer bearer?

Fool?

Giving her directions, he indicated which way to turn toward his boat slip.

His closest neighbor, who lived on a sailboat, watched their progress from his deck.

"Hey, Drew," Marco said, as if he did this kind of thing every day.

"Well, hello there."

"Hello, sir," Phoebe said, apparently polite no matter the occasion. "I'm sorry to intrude on your marina."

"That's perfectly fine," Drew said, fighting back a smile.

"Right here." Finally arriving at his boat slip, Marco took her bag, threw it on deck, then came around and hopped over the stern, holding out his hand. "This part might be a little tricky."

She reached for him and one of her legs managed to

board. But the long torn train of the dress fell into the water, giving up the ghost. This upset her balance, and she clutched desperately for something to hold on to, her hands missing. Damn it all, she was *not* falling again. Not on his watch. He hauled her to him with a firm grip and heard the sound of another loud rip.

For fuck's sake, this dress had to be made out of *lint*.

The wide-eyed look in Phoebe's eyes led him to believe that this tear might be worse than all the others preceding it. He realized this himself a moment later, when his hands touched soft, warm, exposed bare skin.

Her naked back. *Naked*. His fingers tingled like he'd touched a live wire and there went the shimmering again. Naked.

"Oh. Oh gosh." She laughed. "At least I didn't fall in the water."

"I'm sorry about your dress." He swallowed hard. "I didn't mean to ruin it. Guess I don't know my own strength."

"It's fine. None of this is *your* fault."

Glad to hear this bit acknowledged, he let go of her, picked up her bag, and walked down the steps to the cabin to unlock the door.

Marco lived on the marina, not *in* it, so he preferred most of the water to stay outside of his boat. Unfortunately, what was left of Phoebe's dress dragged a whole lot of water in with it. He wondered if he should wring it out, but that would have to be done on deck. For now, he'd have to accept he had a wet bride in his dry cabin wearing a torn dress.

"I must seem crazy to you," she said, clutching the bodice of her dress and staring up at him. "Who does this, right?"

"Someone who *really* didn't want to get married." He opened the door and ushered her inside.

"Yes, yes. You're right." The sound that came out of her reverberated somewhere between a laugh and a sob.

No! He refused to accept a crying woman on his boat, on top of everything else. Hadn't he been through enough today?

"You've come this far," he said cheerfully. "I think you and what's left of your dress can make it. This is an older fishing boat, the kind fishermen used to take out for weeks at a time. Anyway, you can change in the bedroom. Let me know when you're done."

"Thank you." She kicked off her shoes.

Correction: shoe. Marco realized she must have lost one along the way. No wonder she'd been walking funny. The question was when had she lost it, and why hadn't she tossed the other shoe so she could walk evenly? He stopped wondering all of these things when she turned and he got a good look at the gaping opening. Beautiful, peachy skin and the hint of pink panties. He got an eyeful all the way down to the small of her back. He swallowed hard and closed the door.

Look, we're not going there. Not even in the neighborhood.

The truth was, his "rebound guy" status had helped him in the past. Women had this thing about breakups where they believed that the next guy they dated couldn't possibly be "the one." From the moment Marco learned this about women, he decided to be *that guy*. This had worked before, but Phoebe inspired tenderness from him, like a puppy that needed protection.

Desirable and sexy though she was, her groom's body was still warm. Not happening. Nope. It would be wise to get her off his boat, and the sooner the better.

He texted Dylan:

Got held up. Be there soon.

There. Motivation built in. Someone waiting. Marco straightened the cabin, putting away an empty Red Bull and picking up a tee from where he'd tossed it on the ground. It wasn't as if he spent a lot of time on the boat. Just a place to lay his head at night. In some ways, he still thought of the boardinghouse his mother ran in nearby Miracle Bay as home.

"You okay in there?" Marco called out.

She opened the door, dressed in beige slacks and a matching top. The crown had been removed and pieces of her hair stuck out, like there was glue in it.

"Can I ask you something?" Phoebe said.

"Um, sure."

"When I was hanging from the fire escape...you—you said you do this for a living?"

"I meant I'm a firefighter, so I've had a few rescues. Nothing like a runaway bride, though. You're my first."

"Oh, good. I like to think you'll remember me."

"There's little chance I'll ever forget you."

"My father says I have a way of making an impression." She gnawed on her lower lip. "Though I don't think he means it in a positive way."

"You're not close with your family, I take it?"

"I was with my mother. But after she died, my father and I didn't get along too well. Well, I tried. I do love him but can never seem to please him."

"Running out on a wedding he paid a lot of money for was probably also not a good way."

"You're right."

"Sounds like you need to make a plan."

"I do," she said, and he wondered why she couldn't have said those two words in the church instead of here with him where he could easily picture her...doing other things. "But I just need to take a breath and think everything through."

"Any ideas?"

"I have a friend who lives in New York City. I could give her a call."

"That's a long way from home."

Marco couldn't imagine leaving his entire family to go so far away. Then again, the Reyes family had a legacy in the SFFD, which meant everything to him. Being a firefighter in Miracle Bay was his entire identity. He'd tried a brief stint breaking away from tradition but life as a police officer hadn't been a good fit for him.

"New York is a long way from home, but maybe that's what I need, you know? Start over."

"What is it you do for a living?"

"I'm a librarian."

All sorts of sexy librarian images popped into Marco's head and he fought them off with a metaphorical sword. He *refused* to be attracted to this woman. She had real problems.

"Okay, I'm thinking. I might have some ideas."

"I appreciate that, but I probably need to figure this out on my own." She put a hand to her belly. "Do you have saltines or something?"

"You're hungry?"

"Famished. I couldn't eat all day, worried, and wondering how I was going to go through with this. Or how I could get out of it."

"I'm sure I have something."

He busied himself looking through cupboards. At the station, he took his turn in the kitchen and was in fact a favorite.

His meals were fancier there, when he had all manner of fresh ingredients on hand. At home, he cooked for a party of one. This usually meant a can of soup which he always used as a base. He added everything he could get his hands on. For cream of mushroom, mushrooms, of course. Fresh if he could get them. Today he would go old-school. Plain.

The last time he'd added sprigs of basil to a tomato base soup was for one of his short rebound relationships. He wanted to keep Phoebe's soup simple. Uncomplicated. This soup wouldn't keep her here. It would nourish her and give her wings to fly. She'd be gone before he knew it, simply a memory.

After warming up a can of processed clam chowder—kind of a sin in San Francisco—he set it down on the small table in the galley kitchen. "Here you go."

"Thank you." She placed the paper towel on her lap and daintily sipped from the spoon.

She gave him the strange impression of royalty in hiding, like some of those movies that his mother loved to watch. Romantic comedies. Marco didn't see anything funny about them. They were corny and usually ended with two people vowing to love each other for the rest of their lives.

"So, you're a librarian?"

Librarians were sensible. He couldn't picture any librarian he'd ever known hanging from a fire escape.

"Yes, I was an English major and it's about the only job I could find."

"Yeah, not much you can do with that degree."

"Except write or teach. I always thought I'd be a teacher."

"What happened?"

"Oh, my father thought…it wasn't an adequate profession." She knit her eyebrows together and resembled an angel trying to work up a good mad.

Didn't work.

But hell, the man sounded like a real asshole. He already hated him. Who didn't encourage a daughter to be whatever she wanted to be?

"My mother didn't want her sons to be firefighters. Well, she got one out of three. My youngest brother broke away from the family tradition."

"But a first responder is such honorable work."

"So is teaching. My mother thinks firefighting is honorable, but she would have rather me be a teacher. Or an accountant."

His mother's real problem was becoming a widow when her firefighter husband died in the line of duty.

But Marco didn't want to bring up the subject of death after the day Phoebe had.

"And she just accepted what you wanted to do with your life?"

He snorted and crossed his arms. "I didn't give her much choice."

"I think it's harder when you're an only child. I always hated to disappoint my father."

"Listen, I have an idea and I think it could work as long as you're not too picky."

"Not at all."

"My mother runs a boardinghouse not far from here. Maybe you can stay there until you decide on your plan. She has a vacancy. As long as you don't mind sharing a house, kitchen, and bathroom with a bunch of strangers. Think of it as a hostel but a lot nicer. And safe."

"Sounds like an adventure. I'd be up for that. I'll probably meet all kinds of new people."

"The best part of all is that my mother will take payments. Whatever you can give her, whenever you can. Basically, she's a saint."

When Marco was a boy, he used to bring stray animals home. Some of them had been beaten and all had been abandoned.

His mother used to call him "Saint Marco, the patron saint of strays."

And he couldn't help but believe he'd be bringing home another.

CHAPTER 3

"Do you believe in love at first sight, or should I walk by again?" ~ meme

"Look what the cat dragged in." Marco's mother waved him inside. "I can't remember the last time you came over."

"I was just here a few days ago fixing your eternally plugged sink."

"I meant that you never just drop by. Charley and Dylan do." She shot a glance at Phoebe behind him. "Hello, there."

"Ma, this is Phoebe, a new friend of mine." Marco stepped aside. "Phoebe, this is Alice Reyes. Phoebe needs a place to stay for the night, and you have that vacancy."

"Phoebe Carrin—Carrie." Phoebe bowed, then held out her hand. "Phoebe Carrie. How lovely to meet you."

Ah, finally a last name. She sounded formal and that's when he realized what was so different about her. The way she spoke made her sound much older. Her manners were impeccable. She didn't want to "bother him" as she hung from a broken fire escape. She'd called him "sir." Now it was "lovely" to meet his mother. And she'd bowed. Who did that?

"Oh honey, we don't stand on formality here. I'm a hugger!" His mother grabbed Phoebe in a hug, her way with everyone. "I'm Alice Reyes, and this is my boardinghouse. Welcome."

Over his mother's shoulder, Marco mouthed "sorry" to Phoebe, but she didn't seem to mind as she smiled and accepted the bear hug. There was something almost genuinely childlike about her, even though she was clearly educated and bright. Not to mention brave. He didn't know of many women who would have done what she did. Walking out on a church full of people took real courage.

At least she'd be comfortable here for a while. Marco and his brothers had grown up in the three-story Victorian that had been in the family for generations and initially housed only their large extended family. After his father died, his mother and grandmother were forced to take in boarders, and he and his brothers learned to live with strangers. Every few months, someone new would arrive only to leave shortly after. Marco had learned he could make a friend out of anyone.

"Unfortunately, I've already filled that vacancy. A couple signed the lease."

"Damn, I didn't know that," Marco said.

"Maybe you would if you dropped by more often. But anyway, they won't be moving in until tomorrow. Let's go into the kitchen, where we can chat."

She led Phoebe into the large room that served as the center of the home.

"All of the bedrooms are on the upstairs floors but the kitchen is a common area, and so is the great room. There's a computer back there for anyone who doesn't have their own. The password is 'one-two-three-I-love-me.' Simple."

Marco face-palmed. He'd suggested she change that password a dozen times. He followed them into the kitchen, thinking that he should stick around and, later, once Phoebe was situated, let his mother know how he'd found her. Get his mother to keep a close watch on Phoebe. Give her some guidance and advice. She considered herself a spiritual mother, aunt, and friend to all of her tenants.

"It's a beautiful day so as you can imagine, most everyone is out." Mom grabbed a plate of cookies, sat at the farmhouse table, and beckoned Phoebe to do the same.

With one glance behind, she caught Marco's eye, then sat. "You can go. Thank you for your help. I don't want to keep you from your friends."

"No, it's fine. They can wait."

But Marco's phone *was* blowing up. There were text messages from Dylan, wondering where he was. And also one from a recent ex, Veronica:

Hey there. Busy? Come over. I've got news.

He hadn't seen her for weeks, and it was tempting, sure. But he and Veronica had made a clean break. He'd like to *keep* it clean. They'd both agreed his time as rebound guy was done. It was time for her to move on and find "the one," as she referred to her future husband.

In their small enclave of San Francisco, often referred to as Miracle Bay, an odd legend existed. Kiss someone at sunset anywhere in Miracle Bay, and you might find your true love. Residents were divided. Those who believed, believed wholeheartedly. Those who didn't thought the myth was good for tourism and perfectly harmless. Sunset Kiss Day happened to be a big moneymaker for the city. Sailboats were rented and launched, filled with couples hoping to kiss and find true love.

Again, good for business, and no harm done if you didn't believe.

But Marco *believed*. He believed so much the power of the legend petrified him. He'd seen this happen to many of his friends. Dylan was now engaged due to a sunset kiss. Unlike Dylan, who'd "accidentally" kissed his best friend, Charley, at sunset, Marco vowed never to do the same. Accidentally or otherwise.

"And tomorrow is Miracle Sunday, so you're welcome to go with us to the bakery where Charley sells donuts for half price," his mother was saying. "She's my eldest son Dylan's fiancée and she owns Sunrise Bakery."

"She calls it Sunrise Bistro now," Marco corrected.

Mom patted Phoebe's hand and pushed the dish of cookies toward Phoebe. "You know, you look vaguely familiar. Have you always lived in San Francisco?"

"Not really though I love to visit the city."

"Well, maybe our paths have crossed at some point. I never forget a face."

"This place does look a bit familiar, but I've never lived in Miracle Bay. I live..." She hesitated. "South of here."

Wherever she lived, he felt certain it was the wealthier part of the Bay Area. Educated, sheltered, protected. Perhaps by a wealthy and controlling man. Her father.

But he didn't blame him entirely. Phoebe reminded him of a heart that had grown legs and was walking around the city without the protection of a rib cage.

But with her safely tucked away for now, he wouldn't worry anymore.

"THIS IS THE BEDROOM." Alice Reyes switched on the light.

Phoebe paid in cash and had rented a room for the night on the second floor of the spacious Victorian home. She carried only her duffel bag, now stuffed with the remains of her dress. After feeding her and before driving her here, Marco had done his best to help her wring out the dress. Guilt pulsed through her for the shriveled-up gown, a shell of what it used to be. A lot of effort and artistry had been put into this dress, even pearls sewn into the bodice.

She stepped inside the bedroom, taken in by the architecture of the room. The walls were a gentle sky blue, with white crown molding edging between walls and ceiling. Photos of sailboats on the bay, and others of wildflowers. Since her mother had been a bit of an art aficionado, Phoebe checked the artist signatures. No one she recognized, though she admittedly hadn't studied and pursued the arts the way her mother once did.

Phoebe had visited some beautiful places in her lifetime, but she'd always preferred old quaint buildings and original woodwork. She loved the city of San Francisco for all of the older architecture remaining. But too often buildings were renovated, not restored, their character removed.

This home had its own quaint personality. Warm and comfortable, it practically hugged its occupants. If this house could talk it might say: my bones ache and they're brittle, but I still have a lot to teach you. Listen.

"Nothing fancy, but I hope it's homey." Alice ran a hand down the bedspread, a green-and-blue patchwork quilt.

Marco had left, promising to check in with her tomorrow. Phoebe tried to assure him she would be fine from now on, but maybe he was actually worried about his *mother*. He'd just introduced her to a virtual stranger, after all. A wacky one who'd left her groom at the altar.

"I love this. It's just…beautiful." She sat on the daybed with a gold-and-white frame. "I can't tell you how much I appreciate you letting me stay. It was kind of Marco to bring me here."

"Yes, well, he is always saving someone." Alice held up her palm. "Not that you need rescuing, mind you. I'm sure you're fully capable on your own. Maybe you've simply fallen on hard times."

"That's true."

Phoebe's troubles weren't the same as most people, but considering she'd just broken free from her family, she really did have…nothing.

It was a sobering feeling.

She'd never indulged or cared much for bling, haute couture, luxury cars, or yachts. However, she liked to eat on a regular basis. She should be worried, because the world wasn't a kind place to people who had nothing. Instead, she couldn't remember feeling safer than she did at this moment. The last time she'd felt this comforted, this safe, her mother had been alive.

"Would you…care to talk about it?" Alice pressed.

"It's complicated. I had to leave my family. We all…don't always get along since my mother died years ago. There was a big disagreement, and I left."

None of this was a lie.

Alice's eyes rounded in warmth and concern. "Oh dear. Family is everything."

Phoebe worried she'd said too much. She didn't want Mrs. Reyes trying to locate her family and reunite them. She had no idea who Phoebe had been dealing with. Her father might be upset with anyone who had taken Phoebe in. Ethan certainly would be.

She'd lied about her last name, for which she felt horrible, but the name Carrington was well known in the area. She couldn't afford anyone making the connection. She didn't think of it as deceit, but simply protecting these kind people.

Her mother used to have friends like Alice. They'd gone on trips and stayed with people who were of modest means.

She had friends in the Bay Area who hadn't attended elite colleges. They didn't own ten cars and have a live-in maid. Before marrying Phoebe's father, her mother worked in finance and had money, and a life, of her own.

"Family can be everything if you have one that cares for each other," Phoebe said carefully.

"That's true. I don't mean to suggest that every family is a good one. Sometimes, you create your own family." She sat beside Phoebe. "When I was a young woman, I came out to California from Alabama to live with my new husband. I didn't know a single soul at the time. My mother-in-law, Abuelita, you'll meet her tomorrow. She would only speak Spanish to me for an entire year. Did I mention I didn't speak any Spanish? She didn't much care for me. We grew on each other. Now, I'm like her own daughter."

"And your husband? Will I also meet him?"

"I like to think that you'll meet him inside his sons. But no, honey, he died many years ago in the line of duty. A firefighter, just like Marco and Dylan. My youngest, Joe, is the only one who escaped the family tradition of risking life and limb."

"I'm so sorry."

Marco had left out the bit about his father's death, and it sure made sense that his mother would have preferred him choosing a safer occupation.

Picturing Marco without a father reminded her far too much of what it had been like to lose her mother. Obviously, he'd chosen to honor his father by entering the same profession. In a way, Phoebe had tried to honor her mother as well, by marrying a man to support him in his business. In her case it hadn't worked out too well. The love quotient was missing.

Even over a decade later, the passing thought of her mother never failed to engulf her in a wave of grief. Phoebe pushed back the memories of her brushing Phoebe's hair a hundred times every night, and reading from *Harry Potter*, the huge tomes that Phoebe loved. Her mother, taking her on little unannounced road trips, just the two of them, places like a sweet little beach house in Santa Cruz, or Chinatown in the city, where her mother had many friends. Becky Carrington made friends easily, unlike her socially awkward daughter.

See the best in people, honey. Everyone has at least one redeeming quality and you'll find it if you look carefully enough.

And Phoebe had lived by her mother's firm belief in the goodness of people. It was the reason she hadn't seen through Ethan until too late.

"I'll let you get settled in." Alice lowered her gaze to Phoebe's bag. "Is that all you have?"

"Yes, for now. I'll um, send for the rest of my things later."

She opened the bedroom door and pointed. "The shared bathroom is just down the hall. In case of overcrowding, and in a pinch, you can always run upstairs or downstairs. It's difficult to share a bathroom."

"Don't worry about me, I'll be fine."

It was just one night. By tomorrow, she'd have a plan.

AFTER LEAVING Phoebe with his mother, Marco made his way back to Juan's. This time, he got a better parking space. Thanks in part, he liked to believe, to his good deed for the day. Good old law of reciprocity.

He flipped his keys in the air and caught them. "Thank you, Father Suarez."

Juan's was the fire crew's usual hangout where the owner kept it colorful and real. Huge sombreros hung from the rafters. Tortilla chips and burn-your-tongue-off salsa were served up in Aztec orange and bright red painted bowls. A pool table was situated near the back where, over the years, many a pool game had been played. Charley and Dylan against Marco and everyone else.

Nearly a year ago, Marco and Dylan had met up here with their youngest brother, Joe, to celebrate Dylan becoming a silent partner in Joe's new business. Their little brother had finally grown up, now took life seriously, and Surf's Up, the company he owned and ran in Santa Cruz, was growing fast. They'd both worried about Joe spending all his free time on a surfboard or a skateboard. But now he was a new business owner, even making the occasional work trip to Asia. Dylan was getting married, and Marco, well...nothing new there.

Unless he counted the whole bridal rescue today.

Over chips, hot wings, salsa, and cold beer, Marco recounted the story. It was entertaining if nothing else.

"Seriously, I'm not kidding. Her bag hit me over the head when she threw it down from the third-floor balcony."

"Ouch! That could have hurt you badly if it was heavy enough," Charley said. "Are you sure you're okay?"

"Dylan, tell your fiancée not to worry about me. I'm a big boy."

"You tell her." Dylan took a pull of his beer and then brought up Charley's hand to brush a kiss across her knuckles.

These days those two were always wrapped around each other like a burrito. He didn't understand how Dylan suddenly toggled the switch from best friend to lover to fiancé. Granted, he'd known Charley forever. They all had.

"This gives new credence to your black cloud status," Dylan added.

Among EMS personnel, a black cloud was a label given to someone who always seemed to be near the action and in some cases bring it with them. Marco often came on to a shift that had been mostly quiet for days other than the rote medical call. Minutes after he showed up they were called out to a fire or highway multiple-car accident.

"She must have been pretty desperate, poor thing," Charley said, smiling at Dylan but talking to Marco. "I can't imagine ever running out on Dylan."

"Don't even say that out loud," Dylan said.

Marco shrugged. "She has a controlling father. I got that much."

"*Something* is wrong," Charley said. "Running away sends a strong message."

"She must have issues standing up to the old man."

"Speaking of which, do you think Coral would have approved of us?" Charley asked Dylan.

She'd been raised by a controlling foster mother herself, who left the bakery to both her biological daughter, Milly, and Charley.

"Are you kidding? She adored me," Dylan said, pressing a kiss to Charley's temple. "She'd offer to pay for the wedding."

Charley cocked her head, a smile on her lips, and turned to Marco. "Is this girl cute? Pretty?"

There was that whole glowing thing, the electricity in the air. This didn't make sense to Marco at all, and he didn't bother putting it into words.

"Not a girl. A woman. Pretty cute, yeah."

But she wasn't *pretty*, and she wasn't cute. He pictured the hint of pink panties and peachy smooth skin. The more Marco thought about it, the more he had to admit Phoebe Carrie was strikingly...gorgeous. The crown fit. She'd looked like royalty on the run.

"Maybe you should ask her out," Charley said.

"Or maybe she's got enough problems," Dylan quipped.

Marco threw a tortilla chip at his brother. "Well, as much

as I love being the rebound guy, this one is a little *too* close to the action."

"I guess that's true," Charley said. "Unresolved issues and all that."

"Besides I just got out of a relationship, too, and I'm not looking to reconnect with anyone."

"Is that what you call a *relationship*? You and Veronica?"

"Yeah, why not?"

"How long did you date?" Charley held up air quotes on the word "date." "A whole month?"

"So what? It was going well for a month. And then she asked me where she stood. I told her, usually on her own two feet, but she didn't see the humor in that."

"Shocker." Dylan quirked a brow.

"I'm better off single. Women are a mystery."

"There's no mystery. We simply want to be adored." Charley batted her eyelashes.

"Oh, is that all?" Marco deadpanned. "She wants to be the center of my world? The yin to my yang?"

"Why not? Dylan's the jelly to my peanut butter, the pine to my apple."

"Hey, I thought you said *I* was the peanut butter," Dylan said with a snort.

"*Why* do I have to find someone special? Where is it written that a man can't be on his own for the rest of his life?"

"It actually *is* written. It's a song called, 'No Man Is an Island.' Ever hear of it?" This time, Charley threw a chip at Marco.

He caught it and gave her a smug smile.

"What are you going to do with your days off?" Dylan asked. "Got plans?"

"My plans are to sleep. Then maybe eat a little, sleep some more. I might mix it up. Eat then sleep."

"You pulled a long shift. You're owed some DT."

And it had been the shift from hell. Three car accidents with injuries, one house fire, and assistance to one early grass fire in Napa. Zero sleep except short naps. The job was intense, and dangerous, but Marco loved being a firefighter. They were a firefighting family, a Reyes tradition. But because of that, and the nepotism that easily got him hired to the San Francisco Fire Department through an open call, Marco worked harder just to prove himself.

This meant taking every shift he could, volunteering his time, and working harder than everyone else. Frankly, he was exhausted. It was a wonder he hadn't just kept walking and let Phoebe dangle. Or called 911 and let them handle it.

But he flashed back on the whole pay-it-forward concept, and Father Suarez's advice. Marco had a fairly comfortable life. Good things happened to him all the time. A good job doing what he loved, working with his brother, a retired fishing boat suddenly available for rent, beautiful women who thought he was handsome. The list went on. He took on a positive attitude, and he'd been lucky in life, which he conceded made him take too much for granted at times.

But he could no sooner walk away from a rescue than he could stop breathing.

When Charley got up to use the restroom, Dylan crossed his arms and gave Marco the big brother look. "The lieutenant exam is only a few months away."

As if he could forget. Becoming a lieutenant was every firefighter's dream.

"I've *been* studying for months. I'll be ready."

"It's a nice promotion. Better pay."

"Don't worry. I've got this." He gave him a thumbs-up.

As oldest brother, Dylan had fallen into the role of pseudo-father early on. Marco had determined never to cause his brother any more worry than necessary. He helped with Dylan's occasional house flip and woodworking on the odd sailboat or yacht for extra cash. All three brothers saved money because with their mother a widow, they understood anything could happen. She'd battled breast cancer a few years ago, and had fully recovered, but for a while there she'd been one health catastrophe away from financial ruin.

Once they called it a night and Charley and Dylan headed back to their house, Marco drove to the marina. When Charley had moved in with Dylan, into the home the two brothers had shared, Marco had wanted to give those two plenty of room. He'd rented the retired fisherman's boat from one of Dylan's clients. Big enough to house a small crew out to sea for weeks at a time, it had a cabin below with one bedroom, the head, and a galley. He had everything he needed and the whole bachelor pad on the water suited him and his carefree lifestyle.

Marco's neighbor Drew still sat alone on his sailboat as the sunset crested over a foggy horizon.

"How's it going?" Drew called out. "Put out any more fires today?"

"Other than the runaway bride?"

"What was up with that, anyway?"

"She needed help. Took her over to my mother's boardinghouse and that's all I know."

"As always, above and beyond the call of duty." Drew saluted. "A better man than me."

After his divorce, Drew's way of starting over had been to buy a sailboat and live on it. Simple. He rode the train in to work at his job in Redwood City, brown bagged his lunches, and saved every penny for recreation. His own. He was Marco's hero in a way. No encumbrances, no commitments. Every once in a while, a woman.

An old girlfriend had taken one look at Marco's boat and declared Marco "not marriage material." That's when he decided maybe he'd stay here for a while and not bother looking into other rentals as initially planned. This boat spoke for him and it said, "I'm a confirmed bachelor. Happy and settled and there isn't room for a family. No one special, either. Move on. These are not the droids you're looking for."

Sometimes, Marco wondered what it would be like to truly be free. To start over, somewhere new, where there were no grand expectations of him. He wondered if that was exactly what Phoebe Carrie would be doing next. Starting over.

With a groan, Marco sat on the edge of his bed and pulled off his boots. He lay on his back, arms splayed wide, taking up all the room. But as he drifted off to the bliss of sleep, memories of Phoebe slipped in and out of his consciousness.

Hitting him hard enough to bring him to his butt. Straddling him, a look of utter surprise and shock in her eyes. Her peachy soft skin. Pink panties. The way her brow creased when she tried to look mad.

And damn it all, he wished he would stop thinking about Phoebe.

CHAPTER 4

"You had me at hello." ~ Jerry McGuire

When Phoebe woke the next day, the chill of the early morning claimed her, coming in through the cracks of a drafty window. She snuggled deeper under the warm blankets. Surprising herself, she'd had no trouble falling asleep last night.

Granted, yesterday had been an exhausting day. Her failed wedding day. Nerves had prevented her from eating any of the crispy bacon or warm syrup-drenched French toast. Not long after, a few of her eight bridesmaids, Dana, Julie, and her cousin Flannery arrived and set up in the bathroom suite of her father's mansion. Hair extensions, eyebrow mascara, powder, false eyelashes. Phoebe got the works.

"Listen, you probably don't *have* to sleep with him," Dana had said. "I mean, if you don't want to."

"Are you kidding me," Flannery said. "They're getting *married.*"

"They could work up to it." Dana shrugged.

"Good grief. She's not a virgin." Flannery furiously went at Phoebe's cheeks with a brush.

"Cheer up," Julie said. "Maybe he can't get it up. I mean, he's old, right?"

"You're funny." Flannery stopped brushing to take a breath. "Why do you think men invented Viagra? So they can keep up with *younger women*."

"Oh yuck! Viagra could make him go all night. I read one dude had to go to the hospital. I'm so sorry, Phoebe. That sounds awful. But think of the beach house. Aren't you going to Spain this summer? Maybe he'll find a mistress and leave you alone," Dana said. "Something to hope for."

"I don't think he's so bad," Flannery said. "I'd hit that."

"Flannery!" Phoebe snorted.

"What? He's in good shape for a man his age. Trim. Fit. Still has all his own hair, right? And I assume all his teeth. He's got that whole silver fox thing going on. It won't be that bad."

If her friends envied Phoebe because of all the extravagant wedding gifts she'd already received, including a beach house in the south of Spain, they did *not* envy her wedding night. Except for Flannery, apparently.

Blissfully, talk of Phoebe's wedding night steered off into discussions of the brawny and young groomsmen. One of them was Ethan's oldest son, practically the image of him thirty years earlier. Phoebe let her mind drift into the worlds of her imagination. She'd been blessed with a good one early in life. Her mother's influence, probably, due to reading to Phoebe every night. She pictured living on a ranch in the 1800s and being forced into a marriage of convenience with a hot cowboy. Not so bad. But she couldn't help but expect her wedding night to be a disaster. Having such little experience with men, she wouldn't know how to please Ethan, or even if she wanted to.

Wonder what her friends were thinking now? That she'd made a clean getaway, and been braver than any of them would have ever been?

Or maybe Flannery was at this moment making her moves on Ethan.

Phoebe could hope.

Daddy would be so disappointed in her. Once again, she'd failed to be the person he wanted her to be. Someone sophisticated and cosmopolitan. Not a socially awkward woman who couldn't hold down a relationship for long.

She'd almost grown accustomed to Daddy's lack of faith in her. He'd discouraged her from writing and publishing, considering it a career for paupers. Nothing Phoebe ever wanted to do was good enough. But the past several months, since she'd agreed to marry Ethan, had been happy ones. Daddy had been so pleased.

"You're a dreamer, Pumpkin. It's time to get that nose out of your books. And you could do such good work with charitable foundations. You and Ethan complement each other perfectly."

But does he love me? Do I love him? Can I grow to love him?

Is this all there is?

These were all questions Phoebe had about her future marriage. If her mother had been alive, she would have certainly asked her. In fact, maybe she'd have never been in this position at all. But to her father, life was about duty, financial success, and balancing ledgers. He didn't know what to do with Phoebe, who'd always been her mother's daughter. When her mother died, the fun drained right out of him. He'd allowed his older sister, Aunt Sarah, to come to live with them and help raise Phoebe. She'd tried, sure, but it wasn't like having her mother. Aunt Sarah simply went through the motions, but her heart wasn't in it.

Daddy's point was that Ethan didn't need her family's money the way her ex-boyfriend Ted had, or her father's influence, the way that another ex, Leo, wanted. He didn't work for her father, like his junior executive Paul had, a man she dated for two months before realizing he was gay.

Ethan had his own money and influence. And he claimed to need someone with an eye for charitable foundations and the heart for them. Even if this made Phoebe sound like a stock he needed to round out his portfolio, they *should* have been perfect together despite the age difference. Flannery was right. Ethan took good care of himself and looked at least a decade younger.

But if Phoebe couldn't love Ethan, a man so suited for her, maybe she was incapable of loving a man. She understood at the bottom of her soul that she did not love Ethan and never would other than as a friend. And she'd wanted more. Wanted to feel that zing and pop described in books and movies. The connection that left nothing unanswered. *This. This is the one,* her body and mind would say in complete synchronicity. *Him.*

Maybe she'd check her text messages and read about the damage she'd done yesterday. Find out whether there had been a BOLO alert put out on her. Surely the police had better things to do than chase the runaway bride of a billionaire CEO. She fumbled around for her cell, then she remembered that she'd left that leash behind.

Phoebe pulled her slacks and blouse back on. Today she'd shop for some new clothes or maybe hit a secondhand store. Make a bullet list of her plan B.

She tiptoed down the hall and downstairs. First coffee, and then she'd make a plan. She already had her first bullet point.

"Wise men say, only fools rush in but I can't help..."

A melodic, tenor voice wafted from the kitchen and when Phoebe peeked in, she found the source. The man singing leaned against the counter, holding a mug of coffee, until he saw Phoebe.

"Oh, don't stop because of me." She held up a palm. "That was lovely."

"Thanks, sweetie. Just singing to my coffee." He lowered his gaze, gave the liquid a loving look. "Can't help falling in love, you know? I'm Tutti. Can I get you something?"

"Oh, sure. Coffee, please?"

"I'll get it for you, honey. You must be the short-timer. Have a seat. How do you take it?"

"How about a double espresso macchiato with no whip?" He stared at her and she realized she'd done something wrong. "Or...whatever."

"We don't have an espresso machine, sweetie, but I'll suggest it to our esteemed landlord. I meant do you like cream and sugar? I'm going to guess that you do."

"Yes, please."

Before long, the kitchen was filled. A younger couple, his hand tucked in her back jeans pocket, her hand tucked in his. Adorable. There was an older woman with silver dreadlocks, and she and Tutti fought amiably over the coffee. Phoebe met them all: Georgia and Killian, Billy, Liz, Fedora, Kathy, and Tom. She'd never remember all these names. Not that she would have to.

Because she'd be leaving today and still had no idea where she would go.

After grabbing coffee, many spilled into what Tutti called the common area, which was a living room off the kitchen. The couch in there was old and weathered, a colorful yellow-and-red afghan blanket thrown over the back. Phoebe watched as some residents carried their coffee, pastry, or cereal back upstairs with them. Tutti gave Phoebe the lowdown. He showed her which cupboards were individually marked for residents to store their own food, and which areas were shared staple items. Alice bought these on a regular basis and kept the fridge filled.

The bowls and plates were all mismatched but colorful in bright Aztec colors.

On the counter there was a large bottle with both dollars and coins. "This is where you contribute to the fund."

Phoebe stood. "I'll get my money from upstairs."

"You can do that later. You haven't even had any food yet."

"I'm not going to be here after today," Phoebe explained. "I'm probably going to catch a flight to New York soon."

This was all she had for a bullet point list so far. Get as far from here as possible. Clear her head.

"I love New York," Tutti sang. "If I can make it there, I'll make it anywhere."

"Wow, you are *really* good."

"Thanks, sweetie. I'm on my way to the Big Apple someday, too, though probably by way of Las Vegas."

"You're an Elvis impersonator?"

"That I am, among others. Marilyn, Judy, you name it. What do you do for a living?"

"I'm a librarian."

"Kewl. I'm a big fan of the Dewey Decimal System."

"I was supposed to get married yesterday," Phoebe blurted out. Something about Tutti's soulful eyes, his tightly braided dark hair and mocha skin, made Phoebe open up.

Or it might be something about this house. Either way. She spilled her guts.

"I need to start over and I thought I'd go out to New York where I have a good friend. She's in publishing and I've always wanted to be involved."

"And your job at the library? Won't they miss you?"

"I had to quit. Ethan—my fiancé—he asked me to. We were going on our honeymoon for a month and he thought my only job should be as his wife and partner."

"He sounds really *old*." Tutti made a face.

Phoebe giggled. "He kind of is, at least for me. He's fifty-nine."

"Robbing the cradle!" Tutti gasped and comically brought a hand to his neck.

"He's a colleague of my father's."

"Hold on. I need more." Tutti filled his cup and sat next to Phoebe, as if preparing to hear a long story. "Spill. Was this an arranged marriage?"

"Not really. My fiancé does a lot of charitable work and my father sort of played matchmaker."

This was the best way Phoebe could put it, and she realized she was being generous. It was far more like an arranged marriage, yuppie-style, than she cared to admit. She'd liked to believe that sort of thing went out with the aristocracy.

"There you are!" Alice said, entering the kitchen. "We've already been to mass, so whenever you're ready, we'll go down to Sunrise Bakery for Miracle Sunday. Buy one donut, get one half off, and you'll meet Charley!"

Alice seemed so delighted about this Phoebe couldn't help but feel a thrum of excitement roll through her.

An older woman dressed in black and walking with a cane came behind Alice.

"Phoebe Carrie, meet my mother-in-law, Senora Pepita Reyes. Around here we call her Abuelita."

"Nice to meet you, mijita," the elderly woman said in a heavy Spanish accent.

Phoebe stood and curtsied. "Lovely to meet you, ma'am."

"Why don't you bow, Tutti? You could learn something from this young lady." She pointed with her cane. "Manners! They cost nothing."

Tutti rolled his eyes and nodded. "I'll try to remember to bow to you every morning from now on, Abuelita."

"Before we go, can I make a phone call? In all the confusion yesterday, I lost my cell," Phoebe said.

"Of course, dear." Alice led her to a little nook by the open living room. "We're old-fashioned here and still have a landline. Dylan and Marco think it's a good idea. Easier for EMS."

Sliding glass doors led to a patio outdoors. The backyard was narrow but deep like so many older homes in San Francisco. A few residents were outdoors, sitting on folding chairs and the bench of a picnic table.

"Is it okay it I make a long-distance call? I can pay you back."

"No problem. You go ahead." Alice left the room, giving Phoebe her privacy.

She had a great memory for both words and numbers and was able to dial Lorna with no trouble at all.

"Phoebe!" Lorna said. "Are you okay, honey? Where *are* you?"

"You heard." That should not have surprised Phoebe but still, it was quick.

Her father must have been up all night, calling all her friends, as if she were twelve.

"Your father called me. He's so worried about you."

The thought sent an ache through Phoebe, but he hadn't been worried about her when she was about to walk down the aisle. Maybe he could stew in his concern now.

"I couldn't do it. I couldn't marry Ethan."

"Gosh, honey, couldn't you have said that *before* the wedding day?"

"I tried, but each time either Daddy or Aunt Sarah managed to talk me into it. You *know* how convincing he can be. And I do wish I could have married Ethan. Maybe my life would have been easier, but...I don't love him."

"Too bad. Ethan is such a catch."

Wait a minute. Why wasn't Lorna sounding sympathetic? She was now running a thriving small press, thanks in large part to Phoebe convincing her father to invest early and heavily. She was one of Phoebe's oldest friends, the only one left from those early grade school years, and she would have done anything for her. Right now, she could use a little support.

"He's a good man, sure, but not for me." Phoebe took a deep breath. "Hey, remember when we talked about running our own publishing company right out of college? I was going to read through the slush pile and pick out winners. I'd do all the editing and you were going to do contracts and marketing."

"I remember."

"I'm finally free and I'd like to come out to New York. I have a little bit of my own money saved and I need to start over. I'm completely without ties and ready to work hard. My fiancé asked me to quit working."

"Oh no. You didn't."

"I know, I'm an idiot. Now, do you see what I'm up against, and why I couldn't go through with this wedding? Ethan wanted me to be someone I'm not."

"I'm sorry."

"It's okay. A chance to start over fresh. Do you think you might be able to hire me?" When silence stretched, Phoebe kept talking. "I won't ask for much of a salary. Whatever the budget can spare. I know I need to work my way up. But I have my degree in English. I started a reading program at the library that was quite successful."

"You know I adore you, but I can't hire you. The publishing industry is on life support and I'm barely keeping the lights on. Many of us are working from home. Cutting corners where we can. As for slush-pile readers, I have people who do that for free."

"For f-free?"

The old words from her father rang in her ears. *Pumpkin, no one is ever going to pay you to read.*

Every chance he got he'd point out a business article he found reporting on the death of brick-and-mortar bookstores, and the inevitable death of print as everything moved to digital. But for years she'd earned at least a decent salary as a librarian, with benefits included. She should have never given up that job.

"I thought it was worth a try."

"I'm so sorry. And whatever you do, don't move to New York City. It's just as expensive as San Francisco *plus* it's hot and humid."

But they had Times Square and Broadway. Great museums and art, and at least at one time, all the big house publishers. And as Tutti sang, "If I can make it there..."

Well, maybe like Tutti, Phoebe could work up to New York.

"Why don't you call your father and explain why you couldn't go through with the wedding? He'd understand. I'm sure he's worried about you. Maybe if you apologized. He'd take you back with open arms. You might even get your job back if your father makes a big donation."

But Phoebe wanted her job back because she deserved it, not because her father had money. Going back to her father meant going back to another man who only saw her as an extension of himself. If not Ethan, her father would find another suitable mate for Phoebe because he didn't have any faith she could manage on her own.

She'd just have to prove to him that she could.

. . .

When Marco finally got himself down to the bakery for Miracle Sunday, he almost missed out on getting his favorite multigrain muffin.

"You just missed your mom and Phoebe. She's super pretty and so nice. She curtsied when she met me, and said, 'How lovely to finally meet you, Charley.' Wow. It's lovely to meet me!"

"Yeah, she's kind of strange that way. Impeccable manners."

"Abuelita loves her." Charley rang him up.

"Of course, she does." Marco shook a finger. "'Manners! They cost nothing, Marco.'"

"For here or are you going to stick around?"

"I'll take it to go. Thought I'd go check out how Phoebe is doing and if she needs a ride somewhere. She was supposed to decide what to do about the rest of her life by today."

"Right, no pressure. You obviously want to see her again."

"Don't make anything out of it. She's my good deed and I don't want it to fall apart." Marco took his bag and turned, nearly bumping into Father Suarez.

"Aha!" he said. "Young Marco. How are you this blessed Sunday morning? I didn't see you at mass this morning."

"Cut it out, Father. You never see me at mass."

"One still hopes. And prays." He bent his head, the ever-wise priest who sometimes reminded Marco of a Latino Yoda. "Have you done your good deed today?"

Funny, Marco heard: *good deed for today, you will do.*

"On my way right now."

When Marco arrived at the boardinghouse, the new couple was moving in. As with most of his mother's houseguests, these were traveling light. A few boxes, a couple of suitcases. People on their way somewhere else, his mother's boardinghouse a short stop along the path to someplace better. Except for residents like Tutti, who had already figured out there *was* no place better.

Phoebe sat on one of the porch steps and every time someone walked past, she rose, smiled, and curtsied. Then sat back down. While Marco observed from the cab of his truck, she brought her knees up to her stomach and lowered her head.

Uh-oh. This did not bode well. His good deed was unraveling fast. Shutting the door to his truck, he came to sit beside her, bumping her leg. "Hey."

Her fake smile lit up her face. "Hi, Marco. How are you today?"

Unfailing good manners even in the face of her misery. Impressive. "Better than you."

She sighed. "That job in New York isn't going to work out."

"Damn, I'm sorry."

"I talked my father into investing in that company. Now my friend has people read the slush pile for free. That's what I wanted to do but she can't pay me. That was my plan. Now, I have no plan. And I have no home."

"How do you not have a home?"

"Because I let my lease go on a really cute condo. I was going to live with my husband."

Sometimes Marco wished he'd stopped asking questions a long time ago. It just got worse and worse.

He draped his arm around her shoulders in a brotherly move. "Phoebe, have you thought of going back to your father and trying to work things out?"

"That's what my girlfriend thought I should do."

"Maybe she's right."

"Neither one of you understand my father. I'm sure he'd forgive me, but then he'll figure out a way to fix this. *His* way. And he won't listen to me. He'll ask Ethan to please excuse his flighty, irresponsible daughter. My father has absolutely no faith in me. Basically, he thinks I need a keeper. And that's where Ethan came in."

"You'll just need to show him that you can make it on your own."

She brightened. "That's what I'm thinking, too. Do you know that I had to quit my job at the library because my fiancé thought I should? And I did."

Ah, shit. She had no job. No place to live. Suddenly Marco felt low on resources. He couldn't think of a good deed big enough to help.

"I still think you should go home and talk to him. Explain that you want to live your own life, that you insist on a little time to show him you can. Look, how about if I drive you? And if you need me, I'll back you up."

"You would do that?"

Her hopeful smile tugged at his heart. "Yeah, of course I would. I would stand right next to you while you tell him how it's going to be."

"That's okay, Marco. My father's house is in Palo Alto. You've done enough. I'll just take the bus."

"The bus?" Even he didn't ride the bus, not since he'd been fifteen. "Not an Uber? I'll pay, if you're low on funds."

"No, I can't let you do that. And I better get used to living on a budget."

While that made sense, he couldn't see Phoebe on a bus. She probably wouldn't get a seat, too polite to take one when someone else might *also* want to sit down.

"If that's what you want to do, then how about I drive you to the bus stop?"

"Thank you."

It took twenty minutes for Phoebe to say goodbye to everyone at the boardinghouse. They already loved her. Tutti gave her a long hug and kissed her forehead like a papa sending his baby off to summer camp for the first time. Mom hugged her tight and asked her to call or write.

"You can come by anytime to visit," Marco said. "We're not that far from Palo Alto."

"Sure. I will."

"It's for the best. Your father will understand he can't treat you like a child. Just stand your ground. Tell him how it's going to be."

This was supposed to be his good deed for today, but as he pulled up to the bus stop, panic seized Marco. *Wrong.* This was wrong on so many levels. She shouldn't go back to her jerk of a fiancé. She should stay here in Miracle Bay.

But how? Where? Why? Why did it matter to him?

"You sure I can't drive you there? I don't mind."

"That's okay." She slid out of his passenger seat and gave him a little wave. "Bye, Marco. I'll never forget you."

He swallowed hard. They were just words, but they hit his heart like ice-pick daggers. He was fairly sure one of those words had just hit a major artery.

"Bye, Phoebe. Have a good life."

He watched for a moment, smiling as she introduced herself to everyone waiting at the bus stop, offering her hand to each one. Even a homeless guy, carrying a filthy satchel with him. Marco resisted the urge to face-palm.

And with that last look at Phoebe Carrie, Marco drove off, hoping like hell he'd done the right thing.

CHAPTER 5

"I believe in true love." ~ meme

Marco's urge to face-palm turned out to be only the half of it.

His compulsion to go back for Phoebe grew thicker with each stoplight. It intensified as he went up a hill, then back down, easing into the flow of traffic in the city. He broke out in a cold sweat.

"She's a grown woman and okay to be on her own. Her father will take her back, forgive her, and all will be well."

If only he could convince himself of this. But even though Marco believed Phoebe to be far more capable than even she seemed to realize, the raging storm would not let him go. How was she going to stand up to her father and fiancé when she couldn't even stand up to *Marco*? Family, those people you loved more than anyone else, could inflict emotional chokeholds on each other. The annoying need to please while at the same time trying to break away. Been there, done that. Bought the T-shirt.

This is not happening, he told himself as he turned and drove back to the bus stop.

I'm not really getting this involved in a situation where I have little to no control. Even Father Suarez would understand my reluctance.

There's no room on my boat. Tight quarters. Worse, Phoebe found it all so romantic.

But Marco kept driving. It was almost as if a magnetic force pulled him to her. When he pulled over near the bus stop, his constricted chest untightened like he'd just unbuttoned a too-tight jacket. She still sat there, waiting with the others. Not smiling. Staring into space, her little duffel bag on her lap.

His good deed was obviously not complete. He'd taken a wrong turn somewhere. Yeah, that was the problem.

Marco rolled down the window and beckoned her. "Phoebe."

She set her bag down, then walked toward him, eyes bright. "Hi, Marco!"

"Yeah, hi. Listen, I think maybe we were too hasty in this Plan B."

"I was thinking the same thing."

"Okay, go get your bag and get in the truck."

She blinked and hesitated a moment, the most backbone he'd seen her display yet.

She narrowed her eyes. *"Why?"*

There's hope for you, Phoebe. You're learning.

"Because I'm going to help you make a plan. This one, clearly, isn't going to work."

"I don't want you to drive me home. I'm sorry, but I already said that, and I haven't changed my mind." She tipped her chin, looking almost regal.

Yeah, *this* is where you choose to assert yourself.

"No, I'm not driving you home."

"Okay, then."

She returned with her bag but not before first cheerfully waving goodbye to everyone sitting on the bench.

As soon as she shut the door, Marco took off, wanting to put distance between himself and the horrible place where he almost said goodbye to Phoebe forever.

PHOEBE DIDN'T KNOW where Marco was taking her, but anywhere had to be better than home with her tail between her legs. Home to Daddy to *apologize* for having run out on a wedding he'd talked her into in the first place.

Since Marco had dropped her off at the bus stop, she'd been practicing her speech:

Daddy, if it takes me a decade I'll pay for this wedding. But I won't marry Ethan, or anyone else right now. I need to be on my own. I'm going to get a job and an apartment in the city. You're right, people won't pay me to read. But there are other jobs out there, besides my librarian job, that will pay me for my knowledge and expertise. You're going to have to trust me on this.

When Marco had left her at the bus stop, it felt as if her entire world had caved in, as if she would die. Her heart ached like it hadn't since she was a little girl. She already missed a man she'd just met, and it didn't make sense. But she craved him like she did doughy chocolate chip cookies, or the warm, buttery cinnamon toast her mother used to make when Phoebe had a bad day.

"Where are we going?" she asked, relieved she didn't have to keep practicing her speech, rewriting it over and over in her head.

In one speech she was apologetic, in another she was

furious at Daddy for not listening to her reservations in the first place.

"First, let me warn you about something. Life on a boat sounds cool and bohemian. Like a nomadic, free lifestyle. Believe me, I get it. But it's also a lot like living in a tent... with walls."

"What's it like at night? You must get a better view of the stars. Do the seals' cries keep you up all night?"

"They can be loud at times in the distance. But mostly they stay away." As he drove, he gave her a quick assessment. "You probably remember, the living quarters are small."

"Why are you telling me all this?"

"Until you figure something out, or another room is available at the boardinghouse, you can stay with me."

"Oh my gosh! Are you kidding? But I don't want to impose on you. You've already helped me so much."

"Well, I guess I'm not done yet." Though his words were clipped his lips tugged in a smile.

"Thank you. I won't stay too long, I promise."

"You've seen the space. The size of a postage stamp. One small head we have to share. One bed. The table turns into a second bed. That will be your bed. Fortunately, I'm gone a lot, so you'll have the place to yourself. We're going to have to figure out the sleeping arrangements." He cleared his throat.

"I don't mind."

"Maybe you should. You don't know me that well."

She could just hear her father's voice in her ears.

You trust people far too easily. You worry me. Phoebe, not every charity who asks you for money is a reputable one. Do you think it was wise to give that homeless man your money? What if he uses it to buy booze? You haven't helped him, have you?

She tended to trust everyone until they gave her a reason not to. And Marco had given her no reason. If he had intended to hurt her in any way, she imagined he would have done so by now. She'd given him free rein in the first few hours she'd known him, all born out of desperation.

"You have an honest face. And your eyes…they don't look like they *could* lie. Plus, I've met your mother and grandmother. And at the bakery this morning, everyone said nothing but good things about you."

He ran a hand through his hair. "At least this will give you some time to think. You can make plans without the pressure of a deadline. This is only until you're back on your feet, of course."

"And I can look for another job."

"You're going to learn how to stand up for yourself. Grow a backbone. Never let anyone push you around again. Even me."

That puzzled her because she didn't think Marco had pushed her around once. He'd been kind and only trying to help. Marco at least *listened* to her. He had mostly disagreed so far, but still.

"Because of me, you almost got on that bus. That would have been wrong."

"You're right. You *did* talk me into that."

"So, I'm sorry about that. We're going to figure this out."

"*I'm* going to figure this out," Phoebe said quietly.

He blinked. "That's right, you are."

"You were right, though. I don't know much about you. Do you have a girlfriend or someone special who's going to get jealous of our arrangement?"

"Nothing to worry about there."

A man who looked the way Marco Reyes did, who carried himself with such confidence and smooth assurance, a *firefighter hero* for crying out loud, without a *girlfriend*? That could mean one of two things to Phoebe. She didn't think he could be gay like her ex-boyfriend. She'd noticed Marco check her out when she was half naked, her dress ripped in the back. His gaze had lingered a *very* long time.

"I see. You have *a lot* of girlfriends."

Eyes on the road, he turned to her briefly, and gave a smirk. "I guess that's true, but only one at a time. You caught me between."

"I'm surprised you're single at all."

"Well, I work very hard at it." The smirk became a full-on smile.

"You must since Miracle Bay is the most romantic place I've ever heard about. And I've been to Paris."

"Romantic?"

"Yes. Tell me more about this sunset kiss legend."

The wheel jerked and for the first time since she'd met him, Marco appeared shaken. The pallor of his face had turned ashen, like someone had just informed him that he had months to live.

"What? Where did you hear that? Why do you ask?"

"Charley told me about it this morning at the bakery. The neighborhood is known for it. Every week there's Miracle Sunday, and in the summer, Sunset Kiss Day. Sailboats launch. Supposedly, you might meet your true love."

"Did she also tell you women put way too much effort into that belief? They coax their boyfriends into a kiss… exactly at sunset. But what's supposed to happen, anyway? Fireworks? Seriously. Imagine the pressure if you think someone is your fate. What if you kiss them at sunset and it *doesn't* work out? What if you blow it?"

"Then I guess they weren't the right one?"

He scoffed. "You believe in all that true love stuff?"

"Don't you?"

"What I believe doesn't matter. But *you* were going to marry a man you didn't *love*."

Ouch. He had a point. She'd always been a romantic,

expecting a Mr. Darcy type to come straight out of her books to court her someday. To tell her she was perfect *just* the way she was, socially awkward and all. All stupid teenage girl stuff she should have outgrown by now. Still, the Sunset Kiss legend had appeal to someone like her, born with a sense of curiosity and imagination.

"I don't think I've ever been in love, so I don't know what it's like. Maybe I'll try this kiss thing out and see what happens."

"That's a *really* bad idea." Marco shook his head. "You need time to be on your own and figure things out. Not rush right into another rebound relationship."

"You're probably right."

"And stop agreeing with everything I say. But seriously. You, a romantic, were going to marry a man you didn't love. How did you *get* there?"

"You have to understand that ever since my mother died, my father has been overprotective. I'm all he has. I'm his only child and he never remarried. The marriage thing…I've had some horrible relationships. Men who wanted to get to my father through me. He doesn't have a son, so they thought son-in-law might be the next best thing."

She stopped for a beat, gathering her thoughts. Should she tell Marco everything, or would he feel too sorry for her? She refused to be pitiful and it simply wasn't the reality. A pushover, sure. But pitiful? Never.

"Ethan came along, one of my father's business associates. I think my father got it in his head that with Ethan's success in the tech industry, Ethan didn't need money or influence so a marriage to his daughter made all the sense in the world. Ethan wanted a wife to run his charitable organizations and that had some appeal for me."

"And that's all? Your father just put the idea in your head, and you went along?"

"Well, no, I explained that Ethan obviously didn't love me. Also, I didn't love *him*. My father said strong marriages are made out of more than romantic love. I told him that I didn't have anything in common with Ethan, either. My father thought it was because of the age difference and I'd eventually get over it."

"How much older is he?"

"Thirty years."

This time Marco nearly drove through a red light and came to a sudden stop. He reached for Phoebe's arm and like the first time he'd touched her, shimmering waves of gold surrounded him.

But she blinked and they disappeared.

"Are you okay?" he said. "I nearly went through a light. Sorry about that."

"I'm fine."

Simply fine, though she couldn't stop staring at his warm hand wrapped around her arm. Marco had large hands with equally big wrists. On one he wore a tight woven friendship bracelet in bright colors, and she wondered who'd made it. Ex-girlfriend? Best friend? When she lifted her gaze, he was staring at her. For a moment they both locked gazes and the strange glow returned.

Marco removed his hand, snapping her back to reality.

"Your fiancé was thirty years older than you? *Thirty?* Did I hear you right?"

"Yes, that's what I said."

"Your father sure asks a lot of you, doesn't he?"

"But age is just a number. Ethan takes good care of himself. He looks at least ten years younger. My cousin Flannery is half in love with him."

Wait. That sounded like she was defending Ethan. No matter what he *looked* like, he happened to be old enough to be her father. He didn't have to marry Phoebe, could have had his choice of women, but rumor was he liked his women young and "trainable." Yuck.

"Is your fiancé Ethan Bellamy of Bellamy Software?"

"Was," Phoebe corrected and bit her lower lip. "He *was* my fiancé."

"I thought he was already married."

"Divorced."

Phoebe let Marco sit with the knowledge for a while. It appeared he needed the time alone with his thoughts. She'd hesitated to tell him about Ethan for this reason. It might freak him out and make him think he might actually have some of Ethan's associates after him because he'd helped her.

"The guy chasing after you was one of his bodyguards."

"Do you want to take me back right now? Make a quick phone call? I assure you there's no reward money for taking me back. I think that's illegal. And I left by own decision. They can't force me back. If you think you're going to get Ethan to help you, don't let him fool you. He takes everyday people and turns them into corporate drones. If you want a job, he—"

This time the tires squealed as Marco slowed suddenly and turned into a McDonald's parking lot.

"Are you h-hungry?" Phoebe asked.

He parked in a spot, then turned to her, his eyes blazing with…uh-oh…hostility. "What do you think of me?"

"I-I don't—"

"Phoebe, I *have* a job. I happen to love my job and you couldn't pay me enough money to sit behind a desk *or* wear wing tips."

"I'm sorry, I—"

"You must think I'm desperate for money, but I do fine on my own. The reason I live on a boat is that I don't want to be tied down. Not to a house, not to *anyone*, or anything."

"Th-that's not what I thought. I know that most people think of Ethan as intimidating."

"He won't intimidate me."

"I'm getting the idea."

"Listen, I live in the city, so I see a lot of wealth. And fire doesn't discriminate. Everyone's home burns to the ground the same. Whether it's in Pacific Heights, or Miracle Bay."

"Sorry, I didn't mean to insult you. Please forgive me. I don't meet people like you often. Sometimes I don't know how to behave. How to act. It's like I don't know what to do with my hands." She held them up.

His eyes narrowed but this time she caught the hint of a single dimple flashing. He seemed to be fighting a smile.

"You know how when you have to give a speech, but you don't have a microphone to hold. Your hands are…there. Limp. Do you hold them to your side? Gesture with them? Clasp them together? Fist them?"

"You feel awkward." He nodded.

"Yes, around you I do. Sometimes. Around…a lot of people."

"I've been wondering why you curtsy when you're introduced to someone."

She made a little sound between a groan and a sigh. "That's dorky, right?"

"My grandmother calls it good manners. But that's who you are. The curtsying is…cute." He shrugged.

"I'm silly and dorky *a lot*. But you…you're so in control of your life. You call the shots. No one tells you what to do."

"Well, my lieutenant does."

"But that makes sense." She hesitated. "Wait. The lieutenant is your boss, right?"

"Yes." He smiled wider, showing off two dimples, not just one. "Listen. I'm not afraid of Ethan. And I'm not afraid of your father. I don't want anything from either one."

"Okay, okay. I'm sorry I even suggested it."

They sat in silence for a couple of minutes, listening to the sounds of city traffic. Then Marco pulled into the drive-through lane.

"Do you want lunch, public servant style? We're here. Might as well get something to eat."

A few minutes later, they were loaded down with fries, chicken nuggets, and soft drinks. Phoebe's guilty pleasure was nuggets, which her father used to say were the most disgusting way to eat poultry. He was wrong about so *many* things.

When they arrived at the marina, the sailboat on the slip next to Marco was docking.

"Hey there!" the man called out with a wave.

"Need help?" Marco set down the bags.

Phoebe watched as he helped the man she'd seen only in passing just yesterday. There was a lot involved with ropes and the sails. Marco seemed to know what he was doing and before long the man was anchored to his spot.

He hopped off and rejoined Phoebe. "Phoebe Carrie, this is my neighbor, Drew Stewart. Drew, meet Phoebe. She'll be staying with us for a short while, so you'll see her around."

Phoebe offered her hand and curtsied before she could stop herself. Awk-weird.

The middle-aged man quirked a brow and took her hand. "Nice to meet you, darlin'. You'll sure be sprucing up the joint so thank you for that."

"She won't be here for long," Marco explained.

Interesting he felt the need to say that. Phoebe wished he wasn't already trying to get rid of her before she even spent one night on his boat.

"I'm sort of in between places," she added, trying to be supportive of Marco's narrative.

"This is just me, helping out a friend."

"Except we just met," Phoebe corrected.

Drew remained quiet, his head bouncing back and forth between them like the interested viewer of a tennis match.

"We're recent acquaintances," Marco said.

"I would say new friends," Phoebe corrected.

"It's not what it looks like, that's all I'm trying to say." Marco picked up the fast-food bags.

Awareness slammed through Phoebe when she realized Marco was trying to explain they weren't a hookup.

Phoebe waved her hands dismissively and with not a small amount of alarm. "Not at all what it looks like!"

"Good to know because yesterday you were wearing a wedding dress." Drew smirked.

Phoebe laughed a bit maniacally. "Funny story. I'll have to tell you all about it sometime."

"Keep an eye out for her while I'm gone, would you?" Marco said, looking over his shoulder as he walked toward his boat.

They sat on a bench on the deck and ate their food quietly. Seagulls squawked nearby and in the distance a seal barked. The cool sharp wind blew Marco's thick and glorious dark hair. He was heartbreakingly good-looking. The kind of man Flannery had warned her about repeatedly. Good-time Johns, she called them.

No, she didn't believe that was Marco. She might be naïve about men, but Phoebe had an almost sixth sense about him.

"After we eat, maybe I can take my dress down to a consignment shop and exchange it for some regular clothes."

"Hasn't that dress seen better days? It's a hot mess. You think someone wants it?"

"It's a famous designer so it's possible. It could be fixed with some alterations."

"Then I'll drive you."

"Don't you have plans? I mean, you have a few days off, right? What do you usually do?"

"Sleep."

"You're serious?"

"Sometimes I sleep, sometimes I don't. It depends on whether I have a girlfriend how much actual sleeping is going on. Here and there I help my brother with a house renovation or two. We flip houses when we can find them. I'm also studying for the lieutenant exam."

Phoebe was still internally blushing over the sleeping versus not sleeping comment. "We should probably establish some ground rules. I don't bother you when you're studying. And you..."

"Yeah?" he said with a smirk. "Go on, Phoebe."

"Well, I..."

He crossed his arms. "You're going to learn to assert yourself and this is your first test. What is your first ground rule?"

"I, um, well. How about don't look at me when I'm naked."

He went brows up. "That's *it*?"

"It's reasonable."

"It sure is." He shook his head. "And when are you going to be naked?"

"When I'm taking my clothes off, duh."

He squinted. "You're going to need to do better than that."

Oh, the pressure! He seemed to be a rare good guy, doing everything to help her, and she was now supposed to assert herself with him. Make a demand.

One came to her rather abruptly. "I want the big bed, not the one you said turns into a bed."

He stopped chewing on a fry and slid her a slow smile. "We can talk about that."

"No, I...I *insist*."

"Why?" He narrowed his eyes.

"Because you told me to."

"I told you to ask for the more comfortable bed? When?"

"You *told* me to stop letting you, or anyone else, push me around."

He snorted. "You're learning."

CHAPTER 6

"You stole my heart, but I'll let you keep it." ~ meme

For the rest of the day, Marco drove Phoebe around the city. At a consignment shop in the Haight-Ashbury area, she went in with her torn wedding dress and came out with several bags.

If he hadn't seen it with his own eyes, he wouldn't have believed it.

"All that for one torn wedding dress?"

"The dress has actual pearls sewn into it, smarty-pants." She held out her hand. "I also got some cash."

"Looks like I'm in the wrong business."

Next, he took Phoebe to a cellular store where she reported her phone lost and got a new one.

No sooner had she strapped her seat belt on than she turned to him and snapped his photo, then began pushing buttons on her phone.

He scowled after a few seconds. "What was that?"

Phoebe didn't strike him as a woman who thought being with a firefighter was a real score. They were affectionately called "fire bunnies."

"I texted your photo to my cousin. That way if I go missing…well…" She seemed mortified, her cheeks pink. "My father says I trust people too easily. I'm just trying to be street-smart."

"Let me see that." He held out his hand and after a second she gave it to him, somewhat reluctantly.

Someone by the name of Flannery had replied:

Good God! Who is that?

She had added five fire emojis, apparently not understanding how close she'd arrived at his actual profession.

Phoebe had texted:

In case I go missing. Look for this gorgeous face.

Flannery:

A complete stranger? Who are you and what have you done with my cousin?

Phoebe:

I'm starting a new life. More to come.

He handed back the phone, gratified that Phoebe found him…what had she said? Yeah, uh-huh, gorgeous.

"I should be offended but I'd like to see more of this from you. Use every tool at your disposal. You can't trust everyone, Phoebe, especially when you're so unguarded."

He waited while she insisted on walking into several stores in Miracle Bay to ask whether they were hiring. Everyone wanted experience, however, and Phoebe's degree in English literature didn't much matter to the manager of the local sushi house.

"Don't worry, I'll find something."

"It's just the first day. I'm not worried."

But he was a little bit concerned, to tell the truth, because this was all starting to feel very domestic. The worst thing about it all was how natural this seemed. As though it was an everyday occurrence to hang out with a woman as she shopped and applied for jobs. Next thing you know he'd be holding her purse.

There was nothing even remotely *normal* about his new normal. And still there wasn't even a single moment when he considered ditching her. No, he'd had his chance to lose her at the bus stop.

He tried to tell himself it was because Phoebe needed him so much and he had that old hero complex going on. But this was only part of the truth. The rest of the story was that he needed her, too, for reasons that he didn't understand. Except the utter chaos she'd driven through the center of his life like a Mack truck gave him regular bursts of adrenaline and he was addicted.

And let's be fair, she was nice. Beautiful. Spending time with her wasn't exactly like sticking pins in his eyes. Her skin was incredibly silky and smooth, and her smile...every time she flashed it, he felt a kick to his gut. The sweet way she spoke to everyone she met, from the homeless guy to his mother was...endearing.

But this wasn't a relationship and would never be one. First, he wasn't signing up for permanent. Phoebe would never be interested in a casual thing or in a rebound guy. Second, she had to find her way back to her family and he would not intervene with that. Third, before long she would be back to the men in wing tips after she realized that living on a boat wasn't a life for the privileged.

They got back from her errands, and some of his own, late in the afternoon. Marco was tired and beat and thought a shower might wake him up.

"Time to acquaint you with my boat. Our showers come from a water tank. I take short military showers. Basically, I spit on myself and use a little soap. You should do the same."

He bit back a laugh when her eyebrows quirked in surprise.

Yeah, princess. Not what you're used to. No time to condition your hair or whatever else you do in there.

He was exaggerating, of course, but no need to give her reasons to stay longer than needed.

They ate canned soup for dinner again and while Phoebe studied the online job listings, he tried to read with her nearby.

Emphasis on try.

She smelled so damn good.

"Marco?" she asked.

"Hmm?"

"Who gave you that friendship bracelet?"

He held up his wrist. Yep, still there. From time to time, he forgot he still wore the darn thing. But he'd received the gift five years ago and at the time he'd promised his new friend he'd always wear it. With no real timeline on "always," he saw no reason to take it off.

"That's a long story."

"Well, I have time."

"A little girl gave it to me."

As he told Phoebe the story, part of him relived it, too. He could almost smell the gasoline and feel fear grip him. That February rainfall in the Bay Area had exceeded record highs. On a particular stormy night, one of the many accident calls was to a family of four who were trapped inside their flipped Escalade. As police blocked off the road and redirected traffic, Marco and the fire crew worked to free the family. All were wearing seat belts, which had saved their lives.

But both parents had been knocked unconscious and gasoline fumes posed extreme danger. The hazard unit was dispatched, and Marco began to extract the passengers, placing them on backboards with cervical spine collars to get them on an ambulance and move them to the area hospital.

Separating young children from their parents at a traumatic time was always a dicey situation. Marco and Smitty both worked on getting the children out safely, talking to them calmly as they worked. The girl had been fully awake during the entire ordeal. Her long blond hair hung like a curtain over her face and there was a tinge of blood in it from a small cut.

"M-Mommy! G-get me out of there," she'd wailed. "Don't weave me."

Though she appeared school age, she spoke like a much smaller child.

"Hey, honey. How are you? My name's Marco and I'm going to help you out of here. Don't worry, your mom's fine. Let's get you out so you can go see her."

"I p-peed m-my pants," she said, turning her face away.

"This is scary, I know. What's your name, sweetheart?"

"J-Jess."

As she stuttered and stammered in obvious distress, he assessed her vitals. Her blood pressure was good, skin tone and mental acuity great. He began to carefully work the seat belt that kept her in place and upside down.

"You're really tough, you know?"

"I d-don't think so. I'm cwying f-for m-my m-mommy."

"Don't worry, it's okay to cry. I feel like crying, too."

That had made her giggle.

Because the seat belt was stuck, Marco and Smitty worked carefully to cut her out. One hand on her neck to stabilize, she was gently lowered into Marco's arms, and then strapped to the back boards. Minutes later, they were on their way to join Jess's parents at the hospital.

A month later, the family visited the firehouse to express

their gratitude. And Jess brought Marco a friendship bracelet.

"You weaw this," Jess said, shyly handing it to him. "I made it."

"She told me that you talked to her," her mother said. "Because of you, she felt safe. Thank you."

What he didn't tell Phoebe was that the mother explained Jess had developmental delays coupled with acute anxiety and rarely talked to anyone, much less strangers.

To this day Marco wore the bracelet, a reminder that their rescues weren't always about building and house fires. Until Jess, he'd worried that he'd been preoccupied on the specifics of fire, the force of it, and its properties. But as a firefighter, much of his job involved extracting people from automobile accidents and more importantly being one of the first helpful faces they encountered at the worst moment of their lives.

When he finished the story, Phoebe wiped away a tear.

"No, don't do that. No tears."

"It's such a lovely story," she sniffed. "Poor honey. She was scared."

"You asked so I told you. But I don't want you to cry."

"Well, I'm sorry, Marco. If it's alright with you I'm going to get a little teary-eyed right now. It won't kill me." She stood, clearly annoyed, but as with the nature of this damn boat, she didn't have far to go. "And you can't stop me."

Her choices were the only bedroom or the small bathroom. She wound up stomping up to the deck. Their first disagreement. This was going to be interesting. One big fight and someone would have to abandon ship. And it sure as hell wouldn't be him.

He went back to studying, irritated, because damn it all, Phoebe was one hell of a distraction. Someone and something he had not wanted to find.

And he wasn't looking forward to turning this table into a makeshift bed and sleeping on it or trying to sleep with her only feet away from him, her sweet scent torture. Apparently, he couldn't be like Dylan, who'd managed a platonic friendship with Charley for many years. Marco didn't think it was possible to simply be friends with a woman when there was strong interest and basic attraction crossing lines.

Marco loved those lines and crossed them every chance he had. *But not this time.* He would not be her rebound guy. Phoebe was too vulnerable. Too sweet. This was a good thing because he was studying for the LT exam and the last thing he needed was sex with a gorgeous woman. Right.

Even after the sun set, she remained up on deck. He went ahead and took advantage of her absence and changed the table into the bed he'd use tonight. Yes, she'd get the bed she'd asked for, not because she'd demanded, but because his mother had raised him to be a gentleman.

"Oh my God!" she called out suddenly.

The urgency in her tone had him rushing up. "What's wrong?"

She smiled, then gave him her back, turning starboard and holding the rail. "Check out these stars!"

"Yes, they come out every night."

He swallowed thickly, because the only thing he could notice at the moment was Phoebe's form, framed against the brilliant city skyline and sparkling stars. Her hair was so dark that he caught a glint of blue. Some men were attracted to blondes, but he'd always had a thing for brunettes. This one had long legs and the sweetest ass he'd ever seen.

Oh yeah, *the stars.*

"You're spoiled, mister, if you don't appreciate this spectacular show that nature has put on for us."

"True. Some nights the fog is too socked in to do much

stargazing." It was an unusually clear night and if Phoebe hadn't pointed this out, he would have missed it.

Which must mean that lately he'd been spending too much time below deck studying.

"I actually thought maybe you'd seen a shark in the water," he teased.

"A *shark*? What do you mean? Sharks don't come this close to us. There are sharks this close?"

"This *close*? We're in the bay, after all, and that's their natural habitat."

"But...the boats?"

"They've been known to attack them too, in their fury to find dinner. Lots of damage. Terrible."

He was having fun with this now. Because of the soft, ambient moonlight, he'd bet she couldn't see the smile tugging at his lips.

"Oh my gosh, I had no idea!"

"Are you rethinking your living arrangements? Second thoughts?"

"No, I..."

"Yes, you are."

Without much thought, and because according to his mother he could sometimes behave like a fourth grader, Marco placed a firm hand on Phoebe's low back.

"Watch out!"

She squealed and jumped away from the rail. "Eeek!"

Marco hadn't laughed this hard in a long while. He doubled over with it, reveling in the exhilaration and the release of pent-up energy and sexual frustration.

"Not *funny*!"

Phoebe swung a fist and socked him in the stomach. Correction: she tried. Out of instinct and pure reflexes he intercepted her hand. Thought replaced instinct and he didn't bend her hand back to cause pain. Instead, he tugged both the hand, and its owner, to him.

She wound up flush against his chest, her soft body crushed to his. Even in the near darkness he saw the dilating of her pupils reflected in the moonlight. His heart raced and he felt the blood rush from his head to another organ. A most inappropriate organ. *Down, boy*. Every time he touched her felt like a grand mal seizure coming on. Shimmering. Glowing. She affected him in a way he didn't understand and couldn't put into words. She fit neatly against him like she was made for him.

Would you like some salt with that corn, Marco?

Phoebe searched his eyes, unblinking. "Marco…"

He pushed off a stray hair that had fallen over one eye, and his fingers trailed down the curve of her jaw. With one hand on the nape of her neck, he tugged her to him.

What is it about this woman?

Okay. So maybe this is more than a good deed. Far more.

But she's vulnerable. Just left her fiancé at the altar. One day ago. She doesn't need to take up with anyone else until she figures out her life.

No. Not a good idea. He released her.

"Sorry. I'm going to bed."

And with that he forced himself far away from even the idea of kissing Phoebe Carrie.

PHOEBE STAYED upstairs for a while after Marco had gone to bed.

He'd almost kissed her and the memory of his hard body against hers would remain with her for a long time. His strong hands had pulled her in close and tight and she'd sworn the darkness around them…changed.

She'd been around her share of handsome men before but not one of them had ever had this effect on her. *Why?*

Sometimes she'd catch him looking at her with a curiosity and genuine male appreciation. It was a good idea to keep her distance, at least emotionally, since they'd be staying in such close quarters together. But somehow, she felt drawn to Marco in ways she couldn't explain. The happiest moment of her life might have been when he'd come back for her at the bus stop. She'd never forget how he'd rolled down his window and beckoned to her.

He came back for me.

She couldn't allow Marco to think of her as another rescue. She would make her own way from now on, grateful for the temporary stay. She'd been considering, after looking through some of the classifieds online, that she wanted to do something different. There were dozens of positions for personal assistants, which made sense for a large city.

Working for a different kind of business, like travel, or event planning, she would be able to see what else might be out there before deciding to make a permanent career move. Librarian had suited her for years, but she longed to stretch now. Do something entirely different.

She stepped carefully below deck and into the cabin. The lights were out and only a dim view of starlight streamed through a porthole window. Marco lay on the smaller makeshift bed in the galley, his bare back facing outward, covers low on his waist.

In the darkness, Phoebe felt comfortable disrobing only feet away from Marco in the bedroom. She'd told him her only ground rule, but now, she wanted him to turn and watch her. To find her desirable and irresistible. She stepped through the small doorway into the bedroom. As she lowered her shorts and tugged off her shirt, she imagined doing a little seductive dance for him.

Look at me, look, get an eyeful. Here I am, big boy. You don't know what you're missing. Oh, I would love—

"Phoebe."

She dove under the covers half naked.

Okay, I'm not ready for that.

"Um, yeah?"

"While the bay area is full of sharks, they're small ones that are harmless and aren't even the slightest bit interested in people. Or boats."

"Okay."

"Just wanted you to know. You're safe here."

"Thank you, and I'm so sorry I tried to punch you in the stomach."

"I deserved it."

"You didn't. You were just teasing me. I haven't been teased much, so I'm not used to it."

"No little boy teased you in grade school?"

"I think boys generally tease only the girls they secretly like. I'm awkward, remember? I had such awful social anxiety that for a while my mother allowed me to be homeschooled." Phoebe took a deep and painful breath. "In fourth grade my mother decided it was time for me to try school, or I'd never overcome my innate shyness. She encouraged me to always be kind, and I'd find a friend anywhere I went. It worked well for a while, only I didn't always recognize myself as a follower. A pushover. When you go along with the status quo you can acquire a lot of friends who are more like acquaintances."

"A good way to put it."

"What were you like as a boy? I bet you were cute even then."

"You would have hated me. I was the boy who teased the girl I liked. And I liked a whole lot of girls."

"Oh, I remember you. You were the kind of boy I *wanted*

to tease me. Even then I recognized the pretty girls were the ones teased the most."

"I can't imagine you not being pretty even as a child."

Oh, that was sweet.

"I had braces and had to wear the horrible head gear."

"No wonder your smile is so beautiful."

Was Marco flirting with her? He thought she had a beautiful smile.

"I paid dearly for that smile."

"I bet you did."

She settled comfortably under the covers. "Goodnight, Marco."

"Goodnight." There was a long beat of silence. "Phoebe? You smell awfully good."

He was definitely flirting. The awareness made heat pulse through her body.

"Thank you, and so do you."

Ugh.

Why did I have to say that? He was trying to give her a compliment and she should have accepted it like a grown woman. Instead, she had to return it because that's what she did.

She could almost hear him smile.

"Thanks."

"You need to know." The darkness and soft lull of the water gave her courage. "I've never done anything like what I did yesterday. I usually honor my commitments."

"What made you do it?"

She didn't have to consider her answer. "I had to change my life."

"You have to admit, that was a drastic way to do it."

"I know, but maybe this was necessary. Epic, burn bridges style. No going back to the status quo. I couldn't allow anyone to talk me out of it. It was time. For some reason, I have this unnerving need to please people. To please everyone else and leave myself last. I finally had enough."

"Well, if it helps, I wanted the bigger bed. I am not pleased."

"Thank you for letting me win one."

"You're welcome, Princess."

Phoebe lay wide-awake in bed for hours, even after she heard the pattern of Marco's breathing change and saw the slow rise and fall of his chest. She listened to the sound of the water lapping against the pier piles. Somewhere in the distance she heard wind chimes. The night before, she'd fallen asleep immediately. Tonight, sleep wouldn't come even though she felt safe. She had new clothes and a phone. A temporary place to live in a bed a few feet away from a supremely hot firefighter who thought *she* smelled good. Who couldn't believe she hadn't always been *pretty*.

But when it came to feeling safe, the difference between sleeping in a room at his mother's house and on Marco's boat was like comparing a firefly to a roaring fire.

PHOEBE WOKE the next morning to rays of bright sunshine and the smooth noise of an engine. The boat was rocking and swaying. Moving.

Moving.

She jumped out of bed so quickly that she lost her balance and fell to her knees. Good God! Was she being kidnapped? Had Marco's boat been stolen by someone who would ask Ethan or her father for a ransom? If anyone tried that, she would sock them in the stomach. And this time she wouldn't miss.

With effort, she managed to dress without losing her balance and falling. Shortly afterward, the engine cut, and the boat rocked and swayed.

"Marco!" she yelled, balancing carefully to slip on a sandal.

He appeared above, wearing a backward baseball cap. "What's up?"

"I was going to ask *you* that! Why are we moving? What's happening?"

He rushed down the steps, taking two at a time. Phoebe noticed that he wasn't wearing a shirt. Just board shorts. And he was barefoot.

"Time to move and prove this isn't just a tent with walls."

"Why didn't you warn me?"

"Well, Princess, you were out. Snoring."

"Snoring? I don't snore."

"Yes, you do." He grinned, apparently pleased with himself. "Lightly and a little cutesy, but you do."

"No one ever told me that."

He held out his palms. "Hey, I waited for you to get up. But when it was noon and you still didn't wake up after I nudged you, all bets were off."

Now *she* felt like apologizing.

"I didn't realize I'd slept so late. I'm sorry, I couldn't fall asleep last night for a long time. I guess I'm not used to sleeping on a boat."

He brushed past her, smelling of coconut and the wind. "It's a stellar day, the kind we don't get often in the bay. A good time to anchor out." He flashed her a slow smile. "One of the few perks of boat life."

Curious, Phoebe went up on deck and found they were surrounded by water. In the distance, she could see the Golden Gate Bridge. And all around her, shimmering blue skies. It was so beautiful that her breath caught. A sun ray filtering through a particular puffy white cloud reminded her of a band of gold.

The *ring*.

She hoped they'd found it on the hotel bed. Only one way to find out.

"Hi, Flannery. Thanks for picking up."

"I've been thinking that you might call from a burner phone."

"A *burner* phone?"

"Those throwaway phones you see in the movies so that criminals on the run can't be traced. Thanks to you, I've been answering all calls. They must be having a party at the auto warranty renewal place. I answered every one of their lame calls."

"Flannery…the ring. I left it on the hotel room bed. Did they find it?"

"Of course."

"I thought Ethan should have it back."

"Hm, I would have kept it. You're going to need the money. I wouldn't be surprised if Uncle David cuts you off if you don't come back groveling."

"How is he? Is he doing okay?"

"Worried, of course. I told him that you were fine, and simply had a raging case of cold feet. That you'd probably be back and ready to get married in a few days and he should just hang tight."

"But I'm not."

"I say what I have to say. It's not like you gave me much choice. I had to tell him what he wants to hear."

"Right." Phoebe sighed. "It will be up to me to tell him the truth. And I'll face him. Eventually."

"Why haven't you even asked about Ethan?"

"Oh. And how is he?"

"I think he went back to work the next day. He's in China. His people are *good*. They have a spin. The press release they issued was that you've been hospitalized due to exhaustion. Ethan is by your side, taking good care of you. The wedding has been postponed."

"Outrageous!"

"It's not like you're going to come out of hiding and defend yourself."

Ouch. Yes, she *was* hiding instead of facing this problem head-on in the way she should. And maybe she'd done that for far too long. If she'd stood her ground with her father years ago, if she'd have stopped being a pushover, she might not have had to run out on her wedding day.

"You don't know what it's like."

Flannery was one of four children from two different marriages, so it wasn't as if her father had hung all his hopes and dreams on her. Uncle Perry let Flannery do whatever she liked, whenever she liked, and she often did.

"How are you? *Where* are you?" Flannery asked. "And what's that sound?"

"Ocean waves? Seagulls? I'm on a boat."

"Oh my God, are you leaving the *country*? Where *are* you? International waters?"

Somehow, Phoebe was living an even grander adventure in Flannery's imagination.

"I'm not in international waters. Still right here in California."

"Who do you know that has a boat? One of Ethan's friends? One of Uncle David's friends?"

"I…I met someone, and he's been helping me out."

"The hot guy in the photo? Oh, that's smart. I totally support you having a fling. This is what you needed. By the time you're done, you'll be ready to marry Ethan."

"You're not listening. I'm not ever marrying Ethan and I'm not having a fling."

"I know you think you're going to have this grand love affair one day, but sweetie, that's not for people like us.

Check your privilege. It's not fair to have both true love *and* money."

"Listen. I will tell Daddy but wanted you to know first. From now on, I'm taking charge of my life. I'm not getting married. Not now, and maybe never. I'm going to get a job and an apartment here in the city and live life on my own terms."

"That's inspiring and all, but I'd believe it a whole lot more if you had the courage to say it to Uncle David's face."

Double ouch.

"I'm working on it."

After a few more minutes she hung up with Flannery, promising to check back soon, as she had become the only connection between Phoebe and her father. Right now, this was the distance she needed. Later, she hoped, she and her father would find a new way to be a family. In order for them to have an adult relationship he was going to have to learn to let her make her own decisions.

And she'd just given him a crash course in the experience.

Phoebe took a seat on the bench and enjoyed the sparkling view of the bay. Closing her eyes, she tilted her face to the sun and let the rays bathe her in Vitamin D. Though she wouldn't hazard the direction, Palo Alto was somewhere south of here and as the crow flies Phoebe was not far from home. She'd lived in the affluent Silicon Valley town for many years even if it hadn't felt much like home since her mother died.

CHAPTER 7

"True love isn't love at first sight but love at every sight." ~ meme

Marco anchored out every chance he had, but there hadn't been many recently. Too much going on, he hadn't been anxious to impress anyone, and he'd let the stress of the job eat away at him. The pressure to do well on the lieutenant test. The pressure of being the black cloud and bringing the chaos with him. Add to that Marco's need to show his coworkers that he deserved to be on the crew because of his abilities and *not* his last name.

Mostly, things came easily for Marco. He'd been gifted with enough good looks for girls to chase after him. Graduating high school with an above average GPA meant he'd occasionally opened a book. Though he studied, he hadn't struggled academically like his brother Joe. He had a natural athletic ability and played varsity basketball. This had also made passing the physical part of the firefighting test a cinch.

But he worked his ass off most days. Nothing about firefighting was simple or easy.

But today would not be about stress or work. Today he would enjoy the sun and sea with a beautiful, though completely unavailable, woman. Because that unavailability of hers was precisely what he needed and wanted. It kept him alert, made him think "friends" and not "friends with benefits." *Not* a potential hookup. He could do this. Sure. He would stop with any more thoughts of kissing her.

He'd been so close to doing just that last night. Pressing his lips over hers. It would have ruined everything. She didn't need him to further complicate her already tumultuous life. At some point, she'd get a job and settle in to her life. She would have a lot of growing pains along the way. It was his job to stay firmly planted in the friend zone.

For the first time, Marco *could* have a friend of the female persuasion. After all, Dylan had been friends with Charley for years. And clearly Phoebe needed a friend more than she needed a lover. Chances were that a friendship with Phoebe would last a lot longer for him than a romantic relationship. Those had a way of crashing and burning. Too many expectations and pressures. Face it, relationships were too much work.

But if Marco did this whole thing right, Phoebe could always remain in his life. He'd already experienced how difficult it was to say goodbye to her.

He found Phoebe on the deck, long luscious legs drawn up to her belly, chin tilted, pointing her face toward the sun. Good thing he brought the spare cap with him. Unceremoniously, he plopped the orange Giants baseball cap on her head.

"Here, princess. Ever hear of skin cancer?"

"Yes, I have, now that you mention it. But this is a lovely view and I'm only thinking good thoughts."

"Go ahead and think those thoughts while you have full coverage."

"Says the man not wearing a shirt." She eyed him.

"I lathered on sunscreen. SPF 2,000 or something."

She smiled, tucking her hair behind her ears and repositioning the hat. "Gosh, I never figured you to be so…cautious."

"Uh, firefighter here. I know far too much about the human body."

For instance, how some women could fill out a pair of shorts so their round and perky behind looked edible.

He cleared his throat at the thought. "Especially how the body and skin react to intense heat."

"I never thought of it that way."

"Safety first."

"Yes, sir. You actually have a few things in common with my father."

He doubted that very much. Phoebe's father sounded like an idiot.

"Um, Marco, I feel kind of guilty about something, and I have to tell you the truth."

"Oh great. What now? Am I harboring a fugitive from the law instead of a runaway bride?" That would be about his luck. "Tell me now. I have friends at the police department and they'll never let me live this one down. On my headstone, they'll carve: Here lies a sucker from the SFFD."

"Ha, ha. No." She hesitated a beat. "But…my last name isn't Carrie."

He hesitated. "It isn't *Jobs*, is it?"

She made a face and stuck her tongue out. "No. It isn't. My last name is actually Carrington. And my father is David Carrington."

Carrington.

"I'm sorry I lied. You and your family have been so kind

to me. But I didn't want you or your mother to freak out. People feel indebted to my father. He's done a lot of good work in the Bay Area. Funded school programs. I didn't know you or your family that well at first and I couldn't trust that you wouldn't…try to reach out to him. If only to help."

Why did that name sound so familiar? Carrington. It sounded like a name he should recognize, like General Electric and Samsung. Apple and Intel. Google. But he was stumped until he remembered the program he'd installed recently. Anti-virus software. And he'd seen the name on many desktop monitors in high school years ago.

"Of Carrington *Technology*?"

"Y-yes. That's right."

So, her father wasn't Steve Jobs, but he was Steve Jobs *Lite*. The man was probably filthy rich, but Marco also knew that he funded a scholarship at the high school Marco and his brothers had attended. He'd sent hundreds of low-income kids to colleges all over the country.

Phoebe was biting her lower lip. "You're not freaking out, are you?"

"No, but this explains a lot." He sat next to her on the bench. "Your father is a nice man."

"He can be, and I adore him, but he…"

"I get it. Too controlling."

It made sense. The man was probably used to people falling all over themselves to toe the line with the multimillionaire. He'd expect the same kind of devotion from his only daughter.

"It's not his fault. Like I told you, I'm all he has. And I can tell by your expression that you feel guilty about your part in all this. *Please* don't. These were my decisions and I take full responsibility for them. And I'll never allow him to hurt any of the people that helped me."

"I'm not worried."

But this news was shocking and…sobering. He had the daughter of Silicon Valley royalty on his modest boat. His princess nickname for her hadn't been far off. Any thoughts of a hookup faded slowly into the background, even if the temptation had simply been a wisp. It was never going to happen now. She deserved a lot better than a city employee.

Then again, she also deserved to make the choice herself, from among all the wunderkinds closer to her own age. Yikes. He wasn't used to feeling sorry for himself, especially when it came to a woman. But for some reason the fact she would never wind up with someone like him felt like a huge loss.

"Are you okay?" Phoebe asked.

"Just thinking about dinner. Be right back."

He'd gone to the fish market earlier while Phoebe slept. Having never met anyone who could sleep that soundly, he'd given up on waiting for her to get out of bed. He'd nudged her, said her name, then started whistling "Take Me Out to the Ballgame." Nothing.

Looking forward to taking the boat out, and making a nice dinner, he'd bought crab meat and bay shrimp for cocktails, and large prawns for a tomato sauce sauté.

But he should have bought lobster tails. Caviar.

And champagne.

Don't be ridiculous. She's still the same woman you knew a few minutes ago. Nothing has changed.

Except that she'd had every privilege in life given to her and now she appeared to be throwing it all away. Which pissed him off a little bit were he being honest. He also imagined that having every choice in the world available could turn someone into a snob. But Phoebe Carrington was no snob. Not even close. She was sweet and awkward. Socially inept. He was completely puzzled and intrigued.

And he wanted to be neither of those things.

Instead of joining Phoebe on the deck, he chose to stay below and study. She'd become too distracting and he should keep his distance when possible. The boat rocked and swayed with the gentle rhythm of the waves and he became absorbed in his work. He didn't know how long he'd been reading when he heard her shriek his name.

"Shit!" He stood and ran up.

This was no time for the black cloud to follow him.

He was able to breathe again when he saw her standing at the stern, safe and sound. "What the hell happened?"

"Look!" She pointed in the distance. "This is amazing!"

Damn if it wasn't a school of dolphins. For a moment, he simply studied Phoebe's enthralled expression. She had a way of seeing things as if for the first time. Following her cue, he took a moment to enjoy their whistles and clicks, the blue hue of the sky, the soft lull of the waves.

He definitely didn't anchor out enough.

Still, irritation spiked through him because he didn't like even the transient thought that his black cloud had followed him here to his quiet place. His safe zone.

"I thought something was wrong. You didn't have to *scream*."

"Scream? I just yelled for you." She narrowed her eyes. "I had a feeling you'd change when you knew my real name."

"Your name has nothing to do with this."

"You're not worried my father will come after you if I get hurt?"

"Hell, no. *I* don't want you to get hurt. Not because of your father, but because of me."

"Right. Because it's your calling. Your duty."

"Exactly." He hesitated, but thought why not, and decided to tell her the truth. "Also, I'm…well, I might be a little paranoid."

"Oh, you think?"

He shoved a hand through his hair. "Ever heard the term 'black cloud'?"

"I don't think so."

"It's a term used among EMS personnel. Some hospital workers, firefighters, and EMTs think there are some people who seem to bring on all the action. Every time I'm on shift, within minutes we have our first call."

"Like the full moon?"

"Yeah, and I'm the *moon*."

She laughed and waved her hand dismissively. "Get out of here. No way. That sounds superstitious. It can't be true."

"Phoebe, I was walking down the street minding my own business and your bag fell on me. The next thing I know, you're hanging from a broken fire escape."

"Well, that is true, but it wasn't your fault."

"It never is. I don't mind winding up where I'm needed. When I'm on duty, it's my job. And when I'm off duty, it's a good deed."

It sounded so simple. One notable difference today was the sheer panic that gripped him at the sound of her scream. Similar to the moment when he'd left her at the bus stop. Some annoying force swirled around him and threatened to cut off his oxygen every time he worried he'd seen the last of Phoebe Carrington.

WHILE MARCO COOKED DINNER, Phoebe sat on the bench of the deck scrolling through her phone for jobs. Not surprisingly, there were plenty of high-tech positions in the area. Software engineer, quality control, some security guards needed at the social media giant. Nothing for a librarian with an English degree. She could probably walk into any of those companies, drop her father's name, and get a job for which she was unqualified. They'd pay her a salary and parade her out from time to time to drop the Carrington name.

Not in a million years.

Delicious smells of tomato sauce and garlic wafted and joined the calm sound of water and scent of salty ocean air.

She had nothing. No home, no job, but so far within the last couple of days, she'd lived more life than she had in all her twenty-nine years. Today, she'd been on a boat, anchored out, and watched a group of dolphins at play.

Sometimes, it was the little things.

She watched the sunset dip beyond the horizon, wondering how a legend like the sunset kiss got started. Obviously, someone with the kind of great imagination Phoebe envied.

"Dinner!" Marco called.

Oh yum. He wore a backward baseball cap, a loose-fitting white T-shirt, and board shorts.

"This looks delicious."

"I'm a pretty good cook. Kind of a health nut."

"This is *my* kind of health food."

"Everything fresh and prepared with natural ingredients. Healthy doesn't have to mean boring."

He served crab and shrimp cocktails in small saucers, crusty French bread, and pasta with prawns in a rich tomato sauce. They ate quietly for a while, the clinking silverware and distant sounds of the seals their only company. Then Marco picked up a remote, pressed a button, and music wafted through speakers. A song she recognized from her playlist. "Take on Me" by A-ha.

And Flannery called Phoebe a weirdo for enjoying the classics.

"You like eighties music, too?"

"Yeah, stuff my dad used to listen to. Reminds me of him."

She sat with that for a moment, stunned to realize her

own reason was similar. Her mother had loved Lionel Ritchie and the B-52s, an eclectic mixture.

"Marco, can I ask you another question?"

"My mother didn't teach me how to cook. Trial by fire at the station from some of the best cooks I've ever known. Don't tell my mother."

"That's not my question, silly. What do you think? Does the legend of the sunset kiss apply even if people are anchored out like this?"

He squinted. "Why would you ask *me* that?"

"Don't worry. I'm not going to kiss you." She snorted.

"I didn't think you were."

"You look worried. Sorry, but you do."

"It's *you* I'm worried about. I think you're spending too much valuable time on that myth."

"I find it interesting, that's all. And it's not a *myth*. Charley told me all about her and Dylan."

He snorted. "She really can't stop running her mouth, can she? What did she tell you?"

"That she kissed Dylan when he fell asleep watching a movie with her. Turns out she always had a thing for her best friend. It was an accident, the timing of the kiss. Not the kiss itself. But after that, nothing was the same between them. She and Dylan were each other's true loves all along."

"Want to know what I think? I think you like this idea because it's not all that different from what you've already been through. You like that there could be someone already chosen *for* you, but this time someone you haven't met. And you're hoping this time he won't be thirty years older than you." He leaned back, satisfied. "Am I right?"

"Wrong."

She was annoyed by how close he'd come to a smidge of her truth. She loved the idea of romantic love happening simply because it was inevitable. But she'd never again let *anyone,* or *anything* choose a mate for her, be it a person or a myth.

"I'm going to decide *who* I marry and *when* I marry."

"Nah, but wouldn't it be easier if he was chosen *for* you? Like in the sunset kiss?"

"That's just it. I don't believe it's something that's chosen for you. I think it must be something that's always been."

"Yeah, right." He snorted. "Inevitable. True love. You can't help who you love."

"Love is *always* a choice."

"Then why didn't you choose to love your ex?"

The question surprised her. Even now, she had a difficult time admitting that she was going to marry a man because her father thought it was a good idea. Truth be told she'd never loved Ethan. Some people thought it was possible for love to grow but Phoebe had always wanted more.

"He wasn't right for me."

"Yeah, why not, since you claim age is just a number?" He smirked and bit into a crusty slice of bread.

"Ethan funds a lot of charities, but his heart isn't in any of them. They were tax write-offs. He *hated* paying taxes. Once I saw inside his heart, I *couldn't* grow to love a man like him."

He didn't have anything to say to that but simply nodded as if he finally understood. They finished dinner quietly and Phoebe cleaned up while Marco headed above deck.

"Time to park this beast for the night."

The sound of the motorboat as it whirred, the rough rock and sway of the waves, made Phoebe's stomach rumble. To ease that uncomfortable feeling, she joined Marco. A light spray of water kicked up around them. The city skyline view from this angle, at this time of the evening, was breathtaking. Not as many stars shimmered tonight, hidden by cloud cover and fog. Still beautiful enough to make her heart ache.

Marco stood behind the wheel and steered like the

captain of a large ship, gorgeous and roguish. Dangerous. He had the strong arms and physique of a man who worked with his hands. When his dark hair whipped around with the wind, her heart tugged powerfully.

I could fall in love with this guy.

But life had taught Phoebe that next time, she should know a man's whole heart before she fell in love.

CHAPTER 8

"If I had to do it over again, I'd find you sooner
so I could love you longer." ~ meme

Phoebe offered to cook breakfast for Marco the next morning but her attempts at flipping an egg without breaking the yoke failed. It wasn't like she didn't know how to cook the basics. She'd simply become distracted by Marco wearing his uniform. He cut a fine sight dressed in blue wearing a fitted T-shirt with sleeves which strained against his biceps.

But she had to keep her mind on her own future, ecstatic to have scored an interview for a personal assistant position near Miracle Bay. They wanted someone to organize files, help fundraise, run errands, and make appointments. An attractive, reasonable salary, close to what she'd earned at the library. This sounded like something Phoebe could easily do. And the ad she'd found on the job listings website sounded intriguing:

Personal assistant needed.
Must love people.
Please do not apply if you lack imagination.
Will train the perfect candidate.

"We have a few things to discuss," Marco said. "My schedule is crazy, but I should be on for the next forty-eight hours, longer if I get called in as backup. I'll give you my pager number for emergencies only. Since you have an interview and no car, I have a suggestion."

"Great. I'm wide open to suggestions."

"You can use my truck while I'm gone. Drop me off at the station, then come back to get me." When she plated the eggs for him, he glanced at them, then back at her. "You *do* have your driver's license."

"Gosh, of course. You thought I got chauffeured around?"

"I have no idea."

"No, I did not. I have my own car back home. Someday soon I'll have to go get it. I just want this whole wedding disaster to die down first."

"But have you ever driven a *truck* before?"

"No, but I'm sure I can figure it out. How hard can it be?"

From underneath his lashes, he'd given her a look filled with concern. "My truck is paid for."

"I understand, and I'll be careful."

An hour later, after a crash course in Marco's truck and all the many bells and whistles, Phoebe found herself driving down Mission Street to drop him off at the fire station. The garage door of the large brick building rolled up, and she spied a red ladder truck, a few men milling around inside. Just like in the movies.

Marco hopped out of the truck, shut the door, then tapped the hood. "Pick me up in two days unless you hear otherwise."

"I really won't see you at all for two whole days?"

"Not unless you set the boat on fire or fall in the water and drown. Please don't."

"Ha, ha. A little trust?"

"Or you might see me at Charley's picking up donuts."

"What time?"

"Phoebe, I don't know for sure I'll be the one picking them up. We take turns."

Maybe due to her blank stare, he answered with a sigh. "Around six in the morning."

"Okay, maybe I'll see you then!"

"You'll be okay on your own." He walked away, then stopped suddenly in his tracks and turned back. He held out his hand.

She handed her cell to him and watched as he added himself to her contacts.

Oh, thank God.

"Text only if it's an emergency."

He turned his back to her and held up his hand to wave one last time.

Since Phoebe's father taught her to always arrive early to a job interview, she headed toward her appointment. All those shopping trips into the city with Flannery were coming in handy now as she made her way through the traffic. Just when Phoebe worried she might be late after all and would spend the rest of her day looking for a parking space, a car finally pulled out. Sure, it wasn't near her destination, but she'd take it.

A real miracle in Miracle Bay! *A parking spot!*

No way could this day go downhill from here.

Phoebe checked her phone's GPS to determine how far she was from her interview with Miss Dawn Aguilar. With only a few blocks to go, she had plenty of time to walk to her destination.

The brisk morning greeted her with light fog and a cool early summer breeze. Someone honked a horn and another pedestrian yelled. Nearby, smells of fried fish and pasta competed with each other. She was young, single, and living in the city. Not New York City, home of publishing, but a famous city nonetheless. And Phoebe was right in the middle of all the bustle and excitement. The feeling was exhilarating.

But she hadn't walked two blocks before she remembered that San Francisco was a city known for its hills. And those hilly streets felt markedly different when her legs were doing the duty instead of a vehicle. By the time she arrived at the large Victorian home that strongly resembled a mansion, her legs protested at the sight of four steps leading up to a grand porch.

Not another step. I mean it, missy! You can't make us.

Oh, c'mon feet, we can do this.

"Just four more steps," Phoebe grumbled. "We're early. That's good."

She wondered if this job could be assisting a wealthy philanthropist. Not a bad gig.

Outside, there was no sign or marker indicating the name of a business, giving further credence to the philanthropist idea. Two homes down there had been a shingle on the front door for attorneys, but this appeared to be someone's personal home. Phoebe rang the doorbell, which made the low deep sounds of a grandfather clock.

A beautiful redhead who looked like she'd stepped off a runaway in Paris opened the door wearing an A-line black dress.

Dear Lord, where am I?

"You must be Phoebe Carrington." She held out her smooth-as-porcelain hand. "I'm Amanda Sheridan. So nice to meet you."

Phoebe couldn't help herself, she curtsied, then wanted to face-palm. "Hello, um, ma'am. I'm here for the personal assistant job?"

"Yes, I know. Right this way."

Maybe Phoebe shouldn't have made her statement sound like a question. This only made her sound young, tentative, and awkward. Phoebe followed Amanda down a long hallway filled with pieces of art hanging from the walls. Portraits of Victorian women, some walking down the street holding parasols. What struck Phoebe most were all the portraits of sunsets breaking over mountaintops, lakeshores, and oceans.

"Do you have experience as a personal assistant?" Amanda led them into a large parlor.

"I'm a librarian by trade but I've done a lot of administration in the past. I…I worked for charitable foundations."

"That's in some ways right up our alley. Ours is a rather unique business model."

A middle-aged woman entered, her short bob a lovely shock of silver. It suited her olive-toned complexion and the red pop of color on her lips.

"You must be my appointment. You're early."

Phoebe curtsied again. "I'm sorry. Nice to meet you."

"You're sorry to meet me?" Her hand went to her neck, but a smile quirked on her lips.

"I'm sorry I curtsied. A bad habit of mine."

"I think it's lovely," Amanda said.

"She reminds me of you, Amanda," Miss Aguilar said. "When we first met."

"No." Amanda chuckled. "She's a lot more put together than I was."

Phoebe cleared her throat, ready to end the mystery. "The ad didn't mention your type of business. What do you do, Miss Aguilar?"

"Call me Dawn, honey." She strolled to a burgundy couch and patted the seat beside her. "I guess it's time I tell you what we do. It's not something I put in the ad because it can be a little…off-putting to those who lack imagination. Our business is love and companionship."

Holy print books!

I've stumbled into a bordello.

"Um…uh…"

"Look at her face, Dawn." Amanda chuckled. "I've told you not to lead with that."

"I own The Happy Matchmaker." Dawn laughed then splayed her arms wide. "We're matchmakers."

"Matchmakers?" Phoebe didn't think that was still a thing. There were all those e-services now and one barely had to leave home to find a lifelong mate. She pointed to Amanda. "*You're* a matchmaker?"

Phoebe wondered why any man would want anyone else once they'd laid eyes on Amanda. Then again, maybe she was married. Phoebe had noticed a wedding ring, but on her right ring finger.

"You're probably wondering why we do this with all the online dating sites. Our business is exclusive for that reason. We add the personal touch." Dawn made a wide sweep with her hand. "Amanda started her own franchise not long ago. I taught her everything she knows."

"Dawn is nothing if not a shrewd businesswoman," Amanda said. "And if you love people and are interested in helping them, this is the business for you."

"Have you heard of the sunset kiss legend?" Dawn asked. "Unless you're new here, you've heard."

"I'm staying in Miracle Bay, so yes."

"Ah, Miracle Bay." Dawn clapped her hands in delight. "The gift that keeps on giving."

Suddenly all the paintings of sunsets made more sense. And Phoebe could see how opening up a matchmaking business could be profitable in the neighborhood.

"Do you arrange for couples to go on sailboats for Sunset Kiss Day?"

"A mere five percent of our business," Amanda said. "That happens only once a year."

"I appreciate that businesses rake in the money on that one weekend at the end of summer, but we need to operate year-round. A sunset is a sunset, any time of the year."

"We've created a start of the summer event we call the Sunset Stroll," Amanda said. "This is the first year and one of the reasons we're bringing in extra help."

"I'm sorry." Phoebe stood. "I don't think I can take this job but thank you for the chance."

These ladies were basically *capitalizing* on a myth. A legend. At least her father and Ethan sold actual products. It seemed almost sacrilegious to exploit such a quaint tradition based on true love. Phoebe cared too much for the people of Miracle Bay to be paid by someone who took advantage of their love tradition this way. There would be other jobs.

She'd reached the door when Dawn spoke, sounding smug. "I haven't even told you what you'd be doing."

Phoebe turned. "The ad said running errands and filing."

"And that's too *difficult* for you?"

"Of course not. I...just don't believe in exploiting the legend of the sunset kiss."

Phoebe's entire body shook as she spoke. Maybe it was a weird time to assert herself, but she had developed strong feelings on the subject. She could still picture Charley, talking about the legend and how she'd married her best friend. The legend *meant* something to the people of Miracle Bay. Real or not, it was part of the fabric of their neighborhood and its residents. People she had begun to truly care about.

Amanda whispered something in Dawn's ear, and then passed Phoebe on the way out. "It was nice meeting you, honey."

Instead of following her out, Phoebe stood her ground. It might seem like running out in fear if she followed Amanda out. She would stand her ground.

She was done with running.

Phoebe tipped her chin the way she'd watched Aunt Sarah do when she wanted to appear superior. Whenever she was introduced to the elegant wife of a CEO.

The tilt felt awkward but when she'd already curtsied twice, Phoebe had nothing left to lose. "I'm sorry if I wasted your time."

"You *did* waste my time. I'm a busy woman. I own and operate twenty Happy Matchmaker franchises all over the world and I can claim at least two hundred marriages in all my years of doing business. More than three-fourths of them are still married, which far exceeds the national average."

"That's…nice."

"Nice? It's *incredible*! What is it exactly that bothers you about my business? I didn't get the impression you're a snob. Am I wrong?"

Wait. *She said franchises all over the world.*

"So, it's not just the sunset kiss legend you capitalize on? Not only in Miracle Bay?"

"Capitalize?" Dawn threw her head back and laughed. "Amanda was right about you. You believe in true love."

"Of course I do." She straightened. Crossed her arms. "Shouldn't *you*?"

"My goodness. You're even more like Amanda than I realized. When I met her, she was heartbroken over the end of her marriage. *She* believed in true love. Still loves him to this day. It doesn't mean their marriage worked. Love is a tough business, honey. That's why I add in the companionship part. You see, a good marriage is a triangle, and all three parts must stand equally: love, companionship, and *magnetism.*" She made the shape of a triangle. "Magnetism is the final element and simply can't be quantified. If I could bottle it, I'd be a gazillionaire. Look out, Mr. Gates! *But* no one knows or understands what makes two people drawn to each other like magnets. Those who lack imagination claim its pheromones. Basic science. I don't pretend to understand. Think of me as the facilitator."

Phoebe had probably sounded judgmental, making this poor woman go on the defensive about how she made her living. It wasn't as if she ran a *bordello*.

This kind of attitude wasn't like her. "I apologize. I see I've offended you."

"What do you expect when you are ready to walk out on me so quickly?"

"Yes, I see that now. It's not like me to be so rude. I was raised better. I'm...I'm really sorry."

"Fine! You may leave now."

Phoebe bent her head, ready to scurry out like a mouse. She hated herself for it.

"I thought you were someone with imagination, but I've been wrong before." With that, Dawn turned and walked back down the hallway.

Low blow. Phoebe Carrington did not lack imagination! She'd brought a reading program to the library on a budget so tight it squeaked. She was the girl who thought she could be paid for reading, for crying out loud. One thing she did not lack was creativity.

"Miss Aguilar?" Phoebe called out to her retreating back.

She didn't turn, just stopped. Didn't say another word.

In a voice Phoebe hoped did not sound shaky, she cleared her throat. "I'm…if you're still willing to hire me, I'd like to see how this works. Maybe I *can* be of help."

She turned, a big smile on her face. "It's *Mrs.* Aguilar, honey."

CHAPTER 9

"You were always mine. I just had to find you."
~ meme

"Who dropped you off?"

"You're letting someone *else* drive your truck?"

"Is she another rebound deal?"

Marco had no sooner stepped through the garage door than the rapid-fire questions started coming from the crew. He'd expected this since he'd never had a woman drop him off at work. Nor did he trust *anyone else* to drive his truck.

"She's just a friend I'm helping out. Phoebe."

He didn't mention her last name. All information was on a need-to-know basis and they didn't need to know. His phone buzzed in his pocket and he looked at it, hoping Phoebe didn't actually have an emergency.

But no, his mother again. She'd been texting him for the past two days that she had something important to tell him.

He texted back that he'd see her on Sunday for their family dinner as planned. Then he put the phone in his locker where he kept it while on duty.

"The runaway bride?" Dylan asked.

"Don't call her that," Marco said.

"What runaway bride?" Smitty piped up.

Dylan then told the entire story, as if it were his to tell. There were quite a few laughs and chuckles sprinkled in with some gallows-style humor, a fire station specialty. Marco's black cloud status was once more confirmed.

"That reminds me. I'm going to finish *Frozen* before we get our first call," Smitty said. "The black cloud is here."

"Not funny," Marco said.

"Hey, I thought she was staying with Mom," Dylan said. "Didn't you take her to the boardinghouse?"

"She could only stay one night, and Phoebe wasn't ready to go home so she's staying with me."

"On the boat," Dylan deadpanned.

"Yup." Marco waltzed right into the kitchen to check the chores list.

Dylan followed him. "That's close quarters."

"Nothing funny going on, we're strictly friends."

"Yeah, that's also what Dylan said about Charley." Smitty bit into a donut. "And now look at him."

"I hope I *look* happy and satisfied because I am." Dylan gave him a smug grin.

"It's different in my case. We're *really* just friends. She's not interested, I'm not interested."

Wow, it felt natural saying the lie out loud. It didn't matter whether he was interested or not. He wasn't going to start something up with a woman who was *living* with him. The kiss of death.

"Yeah, there's a first time for everything." Smitty clapped

Marco's shoulder. "But congratulations. Your first platonic friendship with a woman."

"They grow up so fast, don't they?" Dylan wiped a mock tear.

"Cut it out." Marco snorted. "Come to think of it, I've been friends with a girl before. Lots of times. What about Charley?"

"It's not the same," Dylan said. "She was my best friend and your friend by default."

"Well, it still worked."

"Because you had zero interest in Charley."

"Why would I be interested in a girl who was hung up on *you*?" Marco gave him a look to indicate the stupidity of that statement, then studied the chores list. "Aw, man. My turn to clean the bathroom?"

"He's got a point, Dylan." Smitty then turned to Marco. "Life sucks, I know."

"You guys are pigs."

After Dylan went home, Marco went about his chore to get it out of the way. Sue him, but he wasn't interested in the seventh showing of *Frozen*.

"Enjoy the quiet while it lasts," Smitty said to the others. "Because we're getting a call any second now."

After cleaning the bathroom, Marco headed to the weight room. He found their rookie, Johnny, there.

"Hey, spot me?" he said from the bench press.

"Sure, buddy."

"So, what's the fascination with *Frozen*?" Johnny said as he lowered the barbell.

"The guys really get into the song where she lets down her hair. When all of it tumbles loose, there's always a standing ovation."

"Yeah, I don't get it."

"Neither do I."

"Hey, so, remember when I took Kate on the sailboat last summer, just for kicks? Damn, I haven't been able to stop *thinking* about her."

"Yeah. Don't fall for the sunset kiss stuff."

"I wasn't, but then this happened. For real, I don't know what to do."

"What's wrong? Just have a good time with her until it's over."

"No, you don't get it." Johnny paused. "She went back to school in Riverside. I haven't seen her since."

From the other room, a cheer arose from the men, which must have meant the hair thing.

"What's the problem?" Marco paused at beat. "Aw, man. You kissed her at sunset, didn't you?"

Johnny groaned and sat up, straddling the bench. "Yeah. She wanted that, and I didn't see the harm in it."

"You're just letting the whole idea mess with your head. Listen, it's simple. The power of suggestion. Right? That's all this is, you know?"

Johnny wiped the sweat from his brow. "Maybe you're right. At first, I thought I was having a stroke. There was like a glow around her, you know? I don't ever get migraines, but…it was like a damn aura. And I felt…electric. And shit, if you repeat any of this, I'll deny it."

Marco blinked.

What the hell was happening to him? He'd gone out of his way to avoid this legend stuff. Glow…shimmer…electric. He could have said those words himself about everything he'd seen from the moment he met Phoebe.

"I'm just going to stop thinking about her," Johnny said.

"Yeah. Yeah, that's what I would advise."

"I feel better already." Johnny fist bumped with Marco. "Thanks, bro."

At that moment, the tones went on for an alarm.

"Damn you, Marco!" Smitty yelled from the living room.

Within seconds they were headed to a fire behind a building near the Mission District.

The apartment complex was one of the few high-rises and fires in them were always dicey situations. But when they arrived, they were directed to the courtyard by some of the residents.

"We tried to stop her," one resident said, shaking his head.

A woman stood by a ring of fire as the flames leapt higher.

She threw in a button-up shirt. "I'm burning everything he ever owned."

"Ma'am, not a good idea," the lieutenant said. "Step away now."

"Just let me throw in the last of his shoes." She tossed a couple of loafers. "There! I'm so sick of men."

Marco put out the fire within seconds, but this lady had bigger problems.

"You have the right to remain silent," an officer said.

"Totally worth it." She rubbed her hands together and held them out to be cuffed.

"Nicole! What the hell. How did you get in my apartment?"

A man rushed to them, poor sucker apparently dressed in the last of his clothes.

"Oh, there he is! Finally showed up. You should have never cheated on me, Randy. Biggest mistake you ever made."

"But we both said no strings! We're supposed to be *casual*." Cradling his head, he surveyed the damage. "What did you *do*?"

"I burned everything you own!" Nicole screeched as the police led her away. "This is for the sisterhood! I bet you *never* string a woman along again!"

"You're crazy!" Randy shouted after her then turned to

everyone else, palms out. "I was supposed to be her *rebound* guy!"

Marco swallowed hard at those familiar words. How many times had he been in a similar position? Despite what Randy may or may not have done, he had the sympathy of every man. They all patted his back as they rolled up hoses and cleaned up.

"There's no such thing as casual," Marco's lieutenant, married twenty years, said. "Don't kid yourself."

When they arrived back to the station, someone was waiting. Every muscle in Marco's body tensed when he recognized the man who had chased Phoebe down the street a few days ago.

"Guys, I'll be right with you," Marco said, as he strode to the curb, still wearing turn-out gear.

The man stood, hands in the pockets of his jacket. He nodded as Marco approached.

"What can I do for you, Ivan?"

If he was surprised Marco knew his name, he didn't react. "As you can see, it wasn't hard to find you."

"I wasn't hiding."

"Good for you. But someone you *met* is hiding."

"You mean Phoebe."

"Exactly."

"And you haven't found her yet, so you're asking me."

"It would be appreciated. She ditched her phone and hasn't used her credit card."

Marco crossed his arms. "Maybe she'll find you if she wants to talk to you."

"She has unfinished business with her fiancé, and he'd like to discuss this matter with her."

"He still considers himself her fiancé? For me, running away on their wedding day is about as big a kiss-off as I can picture."

"Fine. Ex-fiancé." The man snorted. "I see your point. But they obviously need to talk. You know, closure."

"And I'm sure that she'll get a hold of him at some point."

"There's some serious money in this for you if you can help facilitate a reunion. Her former fiancé has plenty of resources."

This was such a cliché that Marco had to laugh. Ask for help from the poor firefighter because *of course* he'll want the money. "Thanks, I'm doing alright."

Ivan shook his head and looked thoroughly disgusted. "At least tell me where you dropped her off."

"At the bus stop. She was going back home."

With that, he gave the man his back and walked inside the station.

THE SCARIEST THING about being alone on a boat at night?

Wind chimes.

They'd been delightful and charming when Marco was here. Now, they were eerie, and foretold of a great and cosmic disaster.

Zombies. On the water. Could zombies swim?

Okay, I'm being ridiculous.

Phoebe had been texting Flannery all evening just to have the mere feeling of having someone nearby. She'd already told her about Dawn Aguilar, and the strange job she'd just been hired to do. She, Phoebe Carrington, was the assistant to a bona fide matchmaker.

Flannery maintained she'd never heard of such a thing except the reality show about the matchmaker who fixed up the very wealthy.

Flannery:

I prefer Tinder where I can actually see the choices.

Phoebe:

Flannery! You're not going to sign up for a dating site, are you?

Flannery:

I use it for fun and not with my real name. My username is Regina Camilla Bananarama.

Phoebe:

And people believe you?

Flannery:

Does anyone even use their real name or picture on these things? Hey, I want you to text me from work tomorrow. Tell me how all this is done. Maybe you'll get to meet some clients.

Phoebe:

I'm not sure they come to her house. She probably has an office...or something.

Phoebe also explained all about beautiful Amanda, who appeared perfectly happy for someone who couldn't be with the man she loved. She did *not* tell Flannery about the shimmering and the glowing she'd felt around Marco. How could she explain this to Flannery, anyway?

Hey, I met a guy and whenever I touch him, he glows and shimmers. No, I'm not kidding.

Yeah, that would go over well.

It was far easier to discuss her new job with Flannery than the strange and intense way she felt about Marco.

Or talk about her father, who according to Flannery, checked in with her every day for an update.

Ethan, for his part, was still in China working some deal. Good thing *he* was bouncing back. Phoebe had already discussed her updated situation with Flannery who promised to relay the information back to her father:

Yes, she was aware she couldn't stay away from home forever.

Yes, she would return soon so they could have an adult conversation about all this.

Yes, she was safe, and he shouldn't worry about her.

Flannery texted now:

Is it scary being alone on a boat at night? I don't think I could do it. You're so brave.

Brave? Phoebe wasn't *brave*. Not when she'd run out on her wedding day.

Good thing Flannery couldn't see the shaking of Phoebe's fingers as she texted back:

It's a little quiet but nothing I can't handle.

Flannery:

Gotta go! Text me later.

Phoebe set her phone down. "You can do this. They're just *wind chimes*."

But a light rain pelted the roof of the boat and the wind now whistled, mixing with the sound of the waves.

She heard steps on the pier and wondered if her imagination was kicking into overdrive. Step, step, step. Then stop. Step. Step. Another stop. Clearly, someone was dragging a body. That had to be it. Oh my God, she was going to witness a crime. Please don't let them dump the body in the bay. If she heard a splash, she'd dial 911.

The steps came closer, and closer still. Phoebe picked up her cell and held her finger above the nine. One more dragging step and she would press. Someone had come aboard! Now they were coming down the steps!

Someone was outside the cabin!

Phoebe pressed number nine, one, and…

"Hello? Marco?"

Phoebe had company. She dropped her cell, unlocked the door, and swung it open. "Hi!"

"Who are *you*?"

"I'm Phoebe, would you like to come inside?"

"Marco used to live here. Did he move overnight?"

"He still lives here."

"Will he be back soon?"

"He's working. It's just me, and I would *love* the company." She held out a hand. "I'm Veronica. Marco keeps avoiding me, but I have great news."

"Well, I always love to hear good news." And face it, at this point, she'd listen to Veronica recite the dictionary.

"How long have you known Marco?" Veronica plopped down on the bench seat in the galley.

"Not long. We just met a few days ago."

"And are you feeling better already?" She smiled broadly.

"What do you mean?"

"I figured if you're here with Marco, something bad probably happened to you." She leaned back, her gaze apprising Phoebe. "Heartbreak? Bad breakup?"

"Well..."

"I thought so. Marco is the best cure for a heartbreak. He makes you feel...I don't know, like you're the center of his world. Oh, he's good. Really good."

Phoebe held up her palm. "I don't think I want to hear this—"

"See, Marco might have a bit of a reputation but he's a good guy. Just don't get too caught up in a romance with him. He'll never settle down. If you want to move on, if you want to see that there's life after a bad breakup...Marco is the best rebound sex you'll ever have."

"I'm not interested in rebound sex. Or any kind of sex."

"Really?" Veronica quirked a brow and scrunched up her nose.

Phoebe cleared her throat. "I mean, sure, I like sex. But Marco and I...we're just friends. I did sort of have a bad breakup and he's letting me stay here for a while."

She nodded. "He does seem to attract the women who need him."

Well, with his looks, no wonder. But now Phoebe understood clearly why Marco didn't have a girlfriend. As he'd said, he had plenty of them. A revolving door, it would seem.

The *rebound* guy.

"What's your good news?" Changing the subject, Phoebe opened the refrigerator and pulled out a water bottle for Veronica.

"Not only did I meet a new man, and he's *perfect,* but I have a new job. Marco is the best luck I've ever had. I wanted to thank him personally. The way I look at it, not enough women give him credit."

Phoebe snorted. "You make it sound like he's a magical genie. I'm sure you would have found someone new and a good job anyway."

"Maybe I'm a little suspicious." Veronica kicked off her heels and uncapped her water bottle. "What about you? What's your story?"

"I left my fiancé at the altar." It came out in a sudden rush of words even though she hadn't planned on telling anyone else. But even Phoebe could recognize girl time.

Veronica didn't speak for one long second, her mouth forming a perfect O.

"I've shocked you." Phoebe laughed.

"Sorry, I've just never met anyone with your kind of courage."

"Courage?"

"Sure. I'd never be able to do it. Make a scene like that?"

"Oh, I didn't make a scene." She probably had but didn't have to see it. "I just slipped out the back. Like...like a coward."

The words stuck in her throat. She *should* have confronted everyone. Maybe sent Flannery to tell them that she wasn't coming. She could just picture everyone gathering to talk sense into her and trying to convince her she was simply a nervous first-time bride.

"It's just the opposite. All that planning, all those people. It takes courage to walk out on all those...expectations."

The words just hung in the air between them.

"I should have said something sooner, but I tried to make it work. The marriage meant a lot to my father."

"Imagine if you'd gone through with the marriage to save face. It makes me wonder how many brides get cold feet but go through with it anyway. You have to wonder if that's why our divorce rate is so high. Maybe more people should run out on their wedding day."

They both laughed at the thought.

"Ever wonder why it seems rarer for a bride to be stood up than a groom? I'm sure some grooms have second thoughts." Veronica pointed between them. "Courage, honey. *Courage*. We ladies have it in spades."

Definitely a rather unique way of spinning the situation, but Phoebe supposed it took some courage to walk out. No matter how she'd done it. In some ways it was the most courageous act she'd ever done. And everything after that moment had been somehow...easier.

"You're right. I don't stand up for myself enough, and I got talked into things I didn't want to do. I went along to make things easier. But that's over now. I started a new life the day I walked out on my fiancé."

"Good for you, girlfriend!"

Veronica and Phoebe chatted for a couple more hours, discussing everything from weddings, to jealous boyfriends, to reality TV, to expensive shoes. And it was just like hanging out with Flannery at their best times, without all the guilt.

By the time Veronica left, Phoebe's relief was palpable. Yes, though she should have ended the engagement sooner, the point was she'd ended it before she and Ethan made the biggest mistake of their lives. A sense of relief loosened inside of her. She didn't *owe* Ethan anything.

Maybe one day he'd even thank her for relieving him from a loveless marriage with an unhappy wife, but best to not hold her breath.

With a restless energy, Phoebe searched for something to do. Something to organize. Marco had a stack of books on a shelf which made her librarian's heart happy. *Know a man's heart when you see what he reads.* Well, okay, then. There were the textbooks he studied. Also some medical tomes like *Gray's Anatomy for Students,* and *Essentials of Firefighting.* But among them, some fiction books as well. Some sci-fi and plenty of John Grisham legal thrillers.

She wasn't surprised not to find any fantasy among them. Well-grounded, Marco wasn't the type given to whimsy. She wondered if he'd ever been in love.

After brushing her teeth and getting ready for bed, Phoebe curled up under three blankets. Though she tried to push him from her thoughts, the scent of Marco lingered, a mix of leather, wind, sunshine, and coconut. An interesting man. The feelings he aroused in her were unlike anything she'd ever experienced but she was still naïve when it came to love and romance. She had a new life to start, and he was her first friend. A good man.

She fell asleep with the wind chimes returning to their more charming tinkling, their sweet melodic sound mixing with the soothing waves.

CHAPTER 10

"Your soul mate will be the stranger you recognize." ~ meme

When Phoebe arrived for her first official day of work at The Happy Matchmaker Amanda wasn't there to greet her. Instead, Dawn, as she requested Phoebe call her, opened the door. She wore a black velvet crushed bathrobe, her silver hair in curlers, makeup already perfectly applied.

"Oh, I'm so sorry! Am I too early?" Phoebe reached for her phone. By her calculations, she was right on time give or take five minutes.

Okay, she was early.

Always be early to work, Pumpkin. Be the first one there and the last one to leave. No one will ever forget you or take you for granted.

"Never apologize for being early, my dear. Were you raised by a military man?" She waved Phoebe in, shut the door, and sashayed down the hall. "I've always loved a military man. Something about that uniform. They never require my services."

"Uh…no."

Today, Phoebe was led upstairs to a large office. The walls were painted a creamy white, with blue edging. Portraits of ships and sailboats and more sunsets were hung with ornate frames. One stained glass window attracted a brilliant ray of sunshine, bathing the room in a holy glow.

Phoebe immediately liked it in here. It smelled like an old library.

"You can start with the box right there." She pointed to a cardboard box in the corner, close to the large and scrolled wood desk. "There's a lot of filing to be done and I need a system. Maybe you can help me with that. I'll be right back, and we can talk more."

Phoebe set down her bag on the desk and began looking through the box. There were photos, both in color and black-and-white along with old receipts, even typed contracts. Everything mixed together in utter chaos. It might be the librarian in her, but she almost broke out in hives. *Precious family photos next to parking receipts?* Holy Dewy Decimal. The poor woman. Before Phoebe could get her organizational groove on, though, the doorbell rang. Thinking that it must be Amanda, Phoebe went to open the door. It wasn't Amanda, but a man dressed impeccably in a pin-striped double-breasted suit.

"Can I help you?" Phoebe asked, putting on her best greeter smile.

"I need to speak with Dawn immediately." Without her asking him inside, he used his tall frame to brush right past Phoebe. "It's of the utmost importance."

"Jeff," came Dawn's voice from behind Phoebe. "I thought we were going to meet at the office."

"I couldn't wait. I have to know. Now."

"Ah, VPs," Dawn said. "Love is not like those hostile takeover deals you people do. It must be done with heart. Finesse."

"That's why I hired you."

"Of *course* you did. It's why you all do." She waved him toward the parlor where Phoebe had been taken yesterday. "Come right this way. I *have* spoken to her."

"Great." The man walked at a fast clip as he followed Dawn down the hallway.

"I'll…I'll be upstairs," Phoebe said to no one as they weren't even listening to her anymore.

She went back to her filing, trying not to eavesdrop, but their voices came straight through the old heating vent grate.

"All you have to do is *tell* her that we're a perfect match."

From what Phoebe could discern, Jeff had apparently met a woman and seemed to be reverse engineering this whole matchmaking thing. He'd asked Dawn to fix him up with her because he'd struck out the first time. Even if this meant Dawn had to seek her out and have the woman agree to be matched by her company, the man seemed to believe it a logical idea.

"That's not how this works," Dawn said, her voice rising in volume. "If you will just trust me, I'll *find* the perfect match for you."

"You don't understand. I've already found her, and I need your help to close the deal."

Phoebe snorted. It sounded like something Ethan would do. Their voices faded after a while as they left the room and Phoebe became lost in creating a filing system. She made notes with suggestions.

There were many photos of couples who were apparently happily matched by Dawn and her Happy Matchmaker franchise. Letters effusive in their praise of Dawn's wonderful skills at finding their soul mate. Invitations to weddings, celebrations of anniversaries. The letters and postcards came from all over the Bay Area...Palo Alto to Marin County.

Phoebe studied a photo of a woman sitting on the tailgate of a blue weathered pickup truck, wrapped in the arms of an incredibly good-looking man. Behind them were rolling green hills and open blue skies. "Mandy and Noah" the back of the photo said, and Phoebe did a double-take, flipping the photo back around. Yes, the redhead was *Amanda,* looking every bit the farm girl. Flannel shirt, worn jeans. Cowgirl boots. A total transformation.

"Yes, that's Amanda," came Dawn's voice as she came up behind Phoebe.

Still holding the photo, she turned to Dawn. "Were *they* one of your matches?"

"Oh, hardly. If I had matched them, they'd still be together."

"What part of the triangle was missing?"

Dawn gave a long and measured look. "You've been paying attention."

Phoebe nodded. "So...which part?"

"Interesting you should ask," Dawn said, moving behind her desk. "They did have every angle. Occasionally that's not enough. That's where family comes in."

"Family? What do you mean?"

"The support of an extended family is absolutely vital to the long-term success of marriages. Had I matched them..." She went hand to chest. "I would have advised against the union."

"But they look so in love."

How could two people do such a good job of faking it?

Dawn waved a hand in the air dismissively. "They're practically a Romeo and Juliet reimagining. Their families hated each other and eventually...well, it didn't work."

Phoebe ached for these two and the Amanda she'd met, now sophisticated and elegant and far from the woman in this photo.

"Don't you worry about Amanda," Dawn said, as if she'd heard Phoebe's thoughts. "She's got a new lease on life and is finally happy."

Except she still wore her wedding ring.

"I have a few suggestions for organizing," Phoebe said, shaking off the emotions the photo brought.

"I'd love to hear them."

"Do you object to having contracts separate from all these letters you've received?" She held up a contract.

"Oh, dear. I guess I have let a few things go over the years. Organization is not my strong suit."

For the next few hours, they worked quietly together as Phoebe stacked and separated, and asked questions about the process of the business. Dawn ordered them both lunch when it was time, catered from a local Italian restaurant.

Apparently, the matchmaking business was quite lucrative.

Dawn dug into her pasta carbonara. "Ask me anything you'd like. I'm an open book."

There was really only one thing Phoebe had to know. "You said you're *Mrs.* Aguilar."

"Yes."

"You're married?"

"I'm sure you're probably wondering where I hide him, right?" She laughed. "Hector is off taking care of our overseas interests. We have a new franchise opening up in Germany."

"Your *husband* is a matchmaker, too?"

At this she laughed. "No, he's our marketing guru. Without him, I doubt I'd have come as far as I have. Now, *we're* a perfect match. Neither one of us is good with organization. We outsourced the accounting long ago."

"How did you meet?"

"Glad you asked. We're a Sunset Kiss match."

Phoebe nearly dropped her fork filled with buttery linguini. A pinch of guilt spiked at the accusation she'd made of Dawn taking advantage of the neighborhood legend. She'd lived it.

"Don't look so surprised. How do you think I got into this business?"

"I didn't know you're actually from Miracle Bay. You made it sound—"

"Those sunsets are not only a testament to the success of my business. I'm a strong believer." She gazed from under lowered lashes.

"I think it's a quaint old-fashioned story, but I wasn't sure I could believe it."

"It's a lot more than a simple story. There's a long history, one only a select few know anything about. I'll be honest. So many times, people don't really care how a legend began."

"You know a lot about this."

"I better. It first happened to my great-great-grandmother. Celeste Ortiz met the love of her life, my great-great-grandfather, on the shores of Miracle Bay. They'd first met as young kids but were separated for decades. They were old-fashioned pen pals who wrote letters on and off throughout the years. Celeste married someone else, and so did Hugo. Neither marriage lasted for long. Hugo went off to war and eventually returned. Celeste had by then opened up a wedding dress shop and began stitching love into every garment. All along they exchanged letters and kept in touch. Late one summer, Hugo arrived in Miracle Bay and wanted to meet with Celeste. But by this time, she was in her forties and assumed true love would never come to her. Due to her long friendship with Hugo, she agreed to see him. They wound up kissing at sunset for the first time and nothing was ever the same. Hugo sold everything he owned and moved to Miracle Bay where he helped Celeste run the shop. They married and had one child rather late in life. That was my great-grandmother. Celeste spread the word about the sunset kiss because she hoped that someday everyone could be as happy as she and Hugo were for the remainder of their lives."

"That's a lovely story."

"Especially because it's all true."

"What's it like? How do you know you're a match after a sunset kiss?"

"I can only speak for myself, but I've heard it on good authority others have also experienced something quite similar. You'll see a glow around the person who's your true love. There will be a shimmering in the air. Electricity. You might feel a magnetic pull to that person, like you can't stand to be physically apart."

Phoebe coughed, wheezed, and reached for her water. She guzzled, while Dawn gave her a raised eyebrow.

A...a glow? How was this even possible? She'd just described everything that had happened to Phoebe from the moment she met Marco. Which couldn't be. This wasn't possible. It didn't make sense at all.

Phoebe cleared her throat and tried to keep her hands from shaking. "So, another question."

"Yes?"

"Is it possible for something similar to happen when you *haven't* kissed someone at sunset? What if you meet someone, and you see a glow around him, and you'd swear sometimes...a sh-shimmer. But what if you've never even *kissed* him?"

"Interesting." She rubbed her chin thoughtfully. "I've never heard of such a thing, but I suppose the mind is powerful enough to make something like that happen if it's exactly what we wish for. You will need to know if the other person sees the same thing. As with all matters of the heart, the sunset kiss can be entirely one-sided."

Oh, wonderful. So, your true love might want nothing to do with you. Talk about the pressure.

"I mean, well, people get married all the time and live happily ever after without the sunset kiss," Phoebe protested.

"Absolutely. Many of my clients, in fact. Sometimes solid and reliable is a lot better than the fanciful stuff. Both have their place. Remember, this is a *Miracle Bay* tradition. Either you're a believer, or you're not. If you're not a believer, there will never be enough proof for you."

But this didn't make any sense. She didn't want Marco to be her true love. He wasn't ready for a relationship and might never be. He was Mr. Rebound with clearly no desire to be anyone else. Not exactly someone she should hitch her wagon to, so to speak.

Anyway, this could all be a huge coincidence. She'd never kissed Marco at sunset, or any other time for that matter.

Which meant that maybe the first order of business was to test this theory out.

With a kiss.

WHEN PHOEBE PICKED Marco up at the station at the end of his shift, something about her was different.

And he wasn't sure he liked it. She seemed…subdued. Too quiet. Unsmiling. He motioned for her to switch places with him so he could drive. Then he had to adjust the seat, and the mirrors.

This is why he never let anyone else drive his truck.

"What's wrong?"

"Nothing's wrong. In fact, you'll be happy to hear I have a

job. The personal assistant interview I mentioned. She hired me on the spot."

"Oh, yeah? That's great, Phoebe. Sure didn't take you long. Good going. I knew you could do it."

"It's an interesting job. I think it might challenge me."

"What does your employer do?"

"She's a matchmaker."

Marco didn't know that was still a thing given Tinder and all the other apps, but leave it to Miracle Bay to have a real, live matchmaker. "Interesting. And what are you going to do for her?"

"Organize. She has *receipts* mixed with photographs. Complete chaos. They desperately need me. You should have seen the disaster. I'm also going to be helping with the Sunset Stroll event they're starting next week."

"Sunset stroll? That's a new one to me."

"Yeah, they wanted an event to kick off the summer."

"Why not? I'm surprised we don't have an Autumn, Christmas, New Year and Valentine's Day one."

"Oh, Valentine's is a great idea! I'll suggest it."

He was half kidding but should have realized Phoebe would run with it. "How did you like having the boat to yourself while I was gone?"

"It's scary at night. But at least I had company."

He nearly drove off the road again. She was entertaining men on his boat? Not okay, but on the other hand, why should he be *jealous*?

"You met someone and brought him back to the boat? My boat?"

"What are you *talking* about?"

"You said you had company."

"Veronica."

Immediately, he pictured everything he owned on fire. "Veronica? You *let* her on my boat?"

"Why not? She was perfectly nice."

"I don't want her over again. If she shows up while I'm out, don't let her in."

"But—"

"No buts!"

Irritation roiling in the pit of his stomach as he drove through traffic like a savage, making it to the marina in record time. If there were damages, he only hoped they would be minimal. He hopped out of the truck and stalked to the boat. It wasn't Phoebe's fault and he had to remember this. She didn't know some women had a mean streak a mile wide. But he'd been a witness to poor choices leading to bad outcomes live and in person. He could have easily been the poor sucker whose clothes and shoes were on fire.

"I don't understand." Phoebe ran after him as he jogged down the pier to his boat slip. "Why are you so upset?"

"You don't know how some women can be."

"Not *Veronica.* She's nice, and anyway I wouldn't have let her damage your boat. And I was with her the entire time."

"Maybe you didn't notice." He hopped on to the boat and automatically held out his hand for Phoebe.

She climbed aboard. "I don't see how but if she did anything, I'll pay for the damages. I promise."

"No, you won't. *She* will."

Obviously, the boat was not on fire. In the bedroom, he flipped through his few clothes and uniforms, looking for tears. Interestingly, his shirts were organized now by color. He didn't remember doing that. Okay, what damage could Veronica have done? Spray paint? *Think, think, think.* He found the few ties he owned and held them up to inspect. The ties were *also* organized by color. He gave Phoebe a look to which she simply shrugged. Nope, no ties were cut in half. No crap in his boots. So far, so good.

He went to the small cabinet in the galley and went

through the spices. Sugar for salt? Oldest trick in the book. Spices were organized alphabetically. An interesting pattern.

"Phoebe?"

"What?" She chewed on her fingernail and wouldn't meet his eyes. "You were gone two days. I was bored."

"You organized *everything*?"

"Everything I could. But you definitely don't have much."

"Because I live on a boat. I don't need much."

"What's this all about, anyway? Why do you think Veronica is crazy?"

"You may not realize this, but some women are vindictive. And crazy jealous." Finger to his temple, he made a swirling motion.

"But she just wanted to give you some good news."

"What *kind* of good news?" A cold shiver went down his spine.

"She met a guy she really likes, and has a new job, too. You're her good luck charm. She's actually very happy for you to have been her *rebound* guy."

Relief swept through him. Okay. This was all fine. Nothing to see here. Occasionally, he let a call get to him, and the one with the burning clothes obviously had. It felt like a slap, like an alarm sounding loudly in a shrilling tone.

His casual dating life was over. Kaput. Fini. Move on.

"Good. That's it, then."

"Is that a service you provide? She seemed to think so."

"I don't provide any services other than ones involving fire, a truck, and a *fire* hose." He scowled.

"That's what she said."

He quirked a brow at the "that's what she said" reference, thinking it would make a good joke, but decided against it. Maybe because this seemed a pivotal moment in his life. As if years from now, he'd be reclining in his Barcalounger remembering this conversation.

Years ago, I used to be the rebound guy for a lot of women getting over a breakup.

Then I met her.

"Let's just say that some women saw *me* as the rebound guy. And…I let them."

She gave him a long look. "Now, that's the truth. But you deserve so much more."

"I'm not sure I do."

"You don't believe that. Maybe you're simply not ready for more than rebound-guy status."

She'd hit on the truth up until the moment he'd met her. Since then, he'd been walking around like he'd been hit over the head with a hockey stick. *Kablam!*

"That's probably true."

"And the women you date feel the same way."

"That's the general idea."

"I can see why this would work for you. Everybody gets what they want."

"Something wrong with that?"

"Not at all. I'm not here to judge you. But I think you deserve better than women taking advantage of your giving nature."

His giving…um, *what*? That's one way he'd never thought of his situation. "I'm not exactly suffering. No one takes advantage of me."

"No?"

"A relationship runs its course. Usually, two months tops and then it's time to move on."

"But why?"

"Why? There's usually nothing left to say or do."

"No sparks?"

He swallowed hard. "No."

There had never been anything of the sort until the day

Phoebe literally *fell* on him. He wasn't even sure "sparks" existed.

She stepped closer. "Marco, I have a favor to ask of you."

"Sure. Anything."

"I want you to kiss me. Just once. I have something I want to check."

He closed his eyes, hearing what he wanted to hear, and also what he resisted. He turned away from her, moving into the galley.

"Anything but that. Phoebe, I'm *never* going to be your rebound buy."

Time to grow up. Learn that every action in life had an equal and opposite reaction. Growing up meant he had to expect consequences. Besides, he didn't want temporary with Phoebe because he'd have to eventually say goodbye. For that, she'd have to remain a friend. Someone he'd have a tough time disappointing.

And still...damn, she was so beautiful and had him feeling things he never had before.

"I don't need a rebound guy."

The galley was small enough that when he turned, he found Phoebe right behind him, and she didn't move quickly enough to prevent her breasts brushing against his chest. He almost hissed at the sizzling hot touch.

She was studying his mouth, not at all bothered by the fact that they were practically hugging they were so close. Phoebe made no move to step back and give them both space.

"Please. Kiss me. Once."

"No." Marco tipped her chin, so she'd face him. "I don't think I could kiss you only *once*. And you were going to take some time and figure your life out."

"Yes. I was. I mean, I am going to do that."

"That's smart." He traced the curve of her face. "You're beautiful, and you don't need someone like me in your life."

"Why not?" He heard such disappointment in her voice that he almost kissed her then and there.

"You...um, because you don't need a man. Any man."

"That's true, but I have a confession to make." She studied his mouth, and a thick blade of desire sliced right through him. "Since the moment we met, I haven't been able to stop thinking about you."

"No, don't say—"

She put a finger to his lips. "Do *not* interrupt me, mister. As I was saying, I *like* you. It isn't just that you've been a good friend to me, and you've been a gentleman every step of the way. But there's also something about you. You're different. Special."

He swallowed hard, still unable to stop caressing her face as she spoke.

But someone would have to threaten to hang him publicly before he'd admit that there was a slight *shimmer* around her.

Still. God help him, he wanted to kiss Phoebe. Hard.

He shouldn't pursue this, but he also didn't see how he'd stop thinking about her when she was around him all the time, smelling so good. Electricity pulsating. Glowing like a ray of sunshine.

Listen to him, sounding like a freaking Hallmark card.

Phoebe was in front of him, reaching under his skin, burrowing deep. At the same time, he didn't want her to leave and give him space. He wanted her to stay where he could keep an eye on her and make sure that no one would think to take advantage of her.

He assumed one kiss couldn't change much of what he'd already been feeling by touching her. And maybe, with any luck, it would end his growing obsession.

She broke the silence. "It's just one kiss, not an engagement."

He cleared his throat. "That's not even funny."

"Do you really believe I'm beautiful?"

"Hasn't anyone ever told you that before? Exactly how many idiots have you dated?"

"Oh...not that many." She studied his mouth.

He gripped her elbows. "What's happening here? For some reason, I feel like I've known you all my life."

Marco tugged her closer. And closer still. He'd kiss her now, and that would be the end of this madness. Because women like Phoebe Carrington hadn't ever been his type. Wealthy and privileged. But also, sweet and innocent without a hint of subterfuge. He was so accustomed to wading through a woman's words to determine what in the world she meant. Phoebe was so open and honest and transparent that she baffled him. He kept expecting "the big reveal."

But she remained exactly the woman he'd believed her to be all along.

"Marco..." Phoebe whispered against his lips. "Please kiss me now."

"You twisted my arm."

He met her lips, angling deeper when the kiss was heady and intoxicating. Sweeter than port wine. There seemed to be no end to this kiss, and she opened for him. He fisted her hair, the strands far softer than he'd imagined. She felt both new and...comfortable. Rocky but smooth.

Easy. And complicated.

He broke the kiss and for a moment they simply stared at each other. Her eyes were wide with surprise. He understood the feeling. This connection was incredible. It felt like a bomb had gone off and they were bathing in its energy. Then they were kissing again, ravaging each other's mouths.

Probing and exploring. Her fingers were threading through his hair.

And all around him this intensity, this buzzing sensation, this damn…*shimmering*. Strangely not disturbing, not even a little bit. It faded to the background and all he felt was the rush of other sensations. Heart pounding and lust throbbing.

Marco's phone buzzed and he ignored it as he ravaged Phoebe's mouth. Those lips were warm and sweet. Soft.

His phone continued to have convulsions and he broke the kiss. He reached past Phoebe to lift his phone and find the name of the person with the worst timing on earth.

He read the text, then frowned.

"I promised my mother I'd come by for dinner tonight. She's been texting me every other day." He put the phone down and met Phoebe's eyes. "Want to come to dinner with a bunch of crazy people?"

CHAPTER 11

"I love you because the entire universe conspired to help me find you." ~ Paul Coelho, The Alchemist.

Even if it had been less than a week, Marco's mother behaved as though her prodigal daughter had returned, and it was time to slaughter the fatted calf.

In other words, the usual.

"Phoebe, dear, I'm so glad you're back!" Mom grabbed Phoebe in a bear hug.

Tutti, flamboyant as ever, seemed ecstatic to see her. "Girlfriend, I see you didn't make it to New York City."

"No, not yet. Plans changed."

"Let's you and I chat." Arm in arm, Tutti led Phoebe out of the room.

"Dinner will be ready in twenty minutes," Mom announced, holding her arm out in a sweeping motion. "Please have a seat in the great room. Chat, drink. Be merry.

Have some of Abuelita's fried plantains. Except you, Marco. You, I have to talk to. In *here*."

Marco followed her into the kitchen. "What's wrong? The sink plugged again?"

"Marco Anthony *Reyes*!" She went hands on hips.

When Mom said his name with an emphasis on the Reyes, he knew he'd done something wrong in *her* eyes. But at thirty, he didn't appreciate being treated like a scolded schoolboy.

He held out both palms. *"What?"*

"You haven't answered my texts! What's the point in my composing all those texts, hunt and peck, letter by letter, correcting autocorrect, wasting *years* of my life, if you're not even going to *read* them?"

"I did read them but I was working. You're familiar with that, right? That thing you do when you have to focus, and your boss gives you an angry look when you're on your cell?"

She pulled a salad bowl out of the refrigerator and started tossing. "Don't give me that. I know how much downtime a firefighter has."

Marco sighed. Not much downtime for him, of course, but he and Dylan had made a pact never to tell their mother that her middle son seemed to attract accidents and fires.

"What's this all about? I came over for dinner. Was there more?"

"Why is Phoebe here? Didn't you find a place for her to stay?"

"Yeah." Marco hesitated for a beat. "She's staying with me."

She stopped tossing the poor salad, which had taken a beating in the past few minutes. "With you. In the *boat*."

"She needed a temporary place to stay. Don't worry, I've been a perfect gentleman."

"Of course you've been a gentleman, that's how I raised

you. But do you now see why living in a boat is not the way to impress a young lady? Just think if you'd been able to offer her a room in a house like regular people."

"I've told you a hundred times. Maybe I don't care to impress a lady. Take me or leave me."

"Oh, I see. That's how it is?"

He nodded, crossed his arms. "That's how it is."

"You don't need to impress a woman. Even Phoebe *Carrington*?"

Considering Alice Reyes had contacts everywhere, he shouldn't be surprised, but still…how had she figured it out? Who'd told her?

"She didn't want to lie to us; she was just concerned that we'd all feel indebted to her father. And she wants to be treated like a normal person. Not like high-tech royalty. That's not who she is."

"What I have to tell you is so much more important than any of that business." She shook her head.

"Spit it out. What's up?"

Mom went back to tossing the salad, more gently this time. "We know Phoebe's mother."

"How could you? She's been dead for years. Phoebe told me."

"Before she died, *Marco*," she explained with an eye roll. "She was here, in our home."

"In…in *our* home?"

"This was before your father died. When only extended family lived with us. Becky was visiting a friend, your father's sister. Tia Marisol."

Tia Marisol had moved to Spain a few years ago and started an art…*foundation*. The pieces were coming together.

"And her little girl was with her." Mom stopped tossing and gave Marco a significant look. "Phoebe."

"Wait. Phoebe has been here before, too?"

"Yes, son. And you two have met."

Shock pierced Marco. He did not expect this at all. He would have remembered someone like Phoebe. Then again, he assumed he'd been a young child.

"Marco? Are you listening to me?"

Oh yeah, his mother was still talking. "Why don't I remember her?"

"Maybe because you were five and far too busy playing with your brothers and cousins to care about our guests." She finished with the salad, washed her hands, and dried them on a paper towel. "Phoebe was only three and cried when your cousin took a toy away from her. You wrenched it out of Alfonso's hands, gave it back, ever so helpful, and bussed her on the cheek. More than anything else, it shocked her into silence. She just looked up at you with those big round eyes."

"No wonder I don't remember. I must have kissed a lot of cheeks since then." Marco chuckled.

"Yes, you were always a little ladies' man. It was very cute. We all laughed, your father fist bumped you, and nobody noticed until later."

"Nobody noticed what?"

Mom faced him. "It wasn't until later that we realized you'd kissed Phoebe during the sunset."

"Big deal. I was just a kid. It doesn't count."

"Maybe it does. Kissing at sunset is not a guarantee of true love, it just opens hearts to the possibility. I see how much time you've been spending with her, and I thought you should know."

"But it doesn't have to mean anything." He cleared his throat. "Right?"

"I don't know. You tell me."

"Do me a favor. Please don't tell her. You'll only freak her out."

"Well, I wouldn't want to freak out two people in the same night."

For the rest of the evening, Marco walked around his mother's house as if he'd been hit over the head with a bat. People talked to him. He simply nodded in what he hoped were the right places. Charley and Dylan arrived, bringing along a cake, some kind of honey-based thing with nuts. Even Joe dropped in, ever the surfer dude, wearing board shorts and a long-sleeved tee. He clapped Marco on the back and said…words. Someone handed him a…something.

Oh, there appeared to be a cold beer in his hand.

Now Dylan was saying…words. "Hey! What's up? You okay there? You're standing by the stove like a statue."

"I'm *fine,*" Marco said, then took a swig of beer. "Can I stand here? Is that alright with you? Is that *bothering* anyone?"

"Defensive much? Sorry, I thought you'd had a bad call on your mind."

"No, just the usual."

"The normal chaos?"

"Yeah."

The backyard bonfire of the poor sap's clothes had been followed by a medical call at a local McDonald's, and two MVAs with one head trauma. He ended his shift with a routine, run-of-the-mill kitchen fire that was quickly under control.

The new shift crew was probably back at the station now, playing poker and rewatching *Frozen* for the one hundredth time.

Damn this black cloud. Would he have ever met Phoebe again without it, or would he have wandered around the rest of his life not bothered by what he didn't even know? Point being, now he knew, and what was he supposed to do with the information? Tell Phoebe that she shimmered, and no wonder, because they'd kissed at sunset and she might possibly be his true love?

Yeah, he'd tell her when hell froze over.

And of course, he hadn't told his mother about the glowing when she dropped the sunset bomb on him. His mother was as true of a believer as anyone in Miracle Bay. But Marco already knew that this sunset kiss wasn't always a two-way street. He'd never wanted the pressure, knowing that if he blew that too, somehow, it might be his last chance at happiness. Ever.

First time he'd admitted that to himself.

Now, he had a headache.

At dinner, he was seated next to Phoebe, still her cheerful self. She laughed and chatted with Tutti and Abuelita, seemingly carefree and unencumbered with life-changing knowledge. He envied her. She didn't know about their shared history and he'd do right by her and not tell her. There was always the chance that he was alone in this.

Knowing her, she might actually believe that she *owed* him. That she should stay with him and live her previously privileged life with a middle-class firefighter. Simply due to the power of a legend. No, he couldn't do that to her. He refused to be someone else who pressured her into staying with them. Someone else who tried to control her destiny. She needed a chance to be on her own and get to know herself. Grow as a person.

Besides, it was too much pressure for anyone to believe that they were soul mates because what if he ruined his only chance? *Her* only chance?

Phoebe gave him a smile, slipped her hand into his, and all reasoning left him. He squeezed her hand, returning the smile. It wasn't her fault that a stupid myth was messing with him. Everything he'd imagined could all simply be the magnetic pulse of sexual attraction. Simple enough explanation.

Everything else, the way his heart raced when she walked into a room, the way he couldn't breathe when he'd tried to say goodbye…all that he would simply have to ignore. Eventually it might pass.

"And so anyway, I'm looking for a server for just one night," Charley said. "In case you know of anyone."

"I'll do it if you can't find anyone else at the last minute," Phoebe said from beside him. "I don't have any experience but I'm a quick study. You all probably know this, but I've started a new job and I'm going to be looking for an apartment in the city. Marco's been nice enough to let me stay with him."

"Yeah, that brother of mine, he is *such* a good guy," Joe said, fighting back a smile.

Marco wanted to wipe that silly grin from Joe's face. Marco wasn't on the prowl with Phoebe. He'd said goodbye to his carefree ways by way of another man's bonfire.

"I'd really appreciate it," Charley said. "It's just one couple and a few businessmen from the area."

"Her bistro is blowing up ever since she got the write-up in *San Francisco's Best Kept Secrets,*" Dylan said proudly.

"It's a good thing I've been working on the menu for a while, perfecting it. Right now, we're appointment only, but that could change soon. I'll probably have to hire an entire staff."

"Maybe even expand," his mother said. "Is your current location large enough?"

"I'd like to stay there as long as I can," Charley said. "It's home."

"A lot of history there," Dylan said, and they smiled at each other.

Everyone in this room, other than Phoebe, was part of that history but none more than those two.

"As long as you don't mind that I don't have any experience, I'm willing to help out," Phoebe piped in. "I'll be working during the days but I'm free nights."

"I may just take you up on that." Charley slid her phone across the table. "Put your number in here and I'll call you if I need you."

"What kind of work are you doing now?" Marco's mother asked.

"I've been hired as a personal assistant to the Happy Matchmaker."

"What's the *Happy Matchmaker*?" Charley asked.

"Believe it or not, it's an old-fashioned matchmaking service, not far from Miracle Bay," Phoebe said. "The owner needed help with an event she's organizing. It's the first annual Sunset Stroll."

"We're the perfect place for a matchmaker," his mother said. "Not sure why I haven't heard of her."

"Yes, you have, mija," Abuelita interrupted. "That's Juanita's granddaughter, Aurora. But she goes by Dawn now."

"Oh, is that her? I thought she was a real estate agent."

"They participate in Sunset Kiss Day but that's only a small part of their business," Phoebe said. "I learned the entire history of the sunset kiss through her."

"I've always wondered how that started." Charley leaned forward.

This was exactly what Marco would like to avoid. More talk of the sunset kiss. He considered interrupting with a joke in order to change the subject, but Phoebe was already on a roll. She told the story of two people who were separated by distance and circumstances for years. How they'd eventually reconnected, after failed marriages to others, kissed at sunset, and went on to live happily ever after.

Even he was a little moved by the second-chance romance. And also spooked. If anyone had paid attention, this was a perfect example of how something "fated" could go horribly wrong. He'd zoned into the "married to other people" business immediately and wondered whether anyone else had. No matter how you spun this tale, it wasn't a happy story in his humble opinion.

There were tears in Charley's eyes. "What a beautiful story. It's never too late for love."

"You hear that, Ma?" Dylan said with a smirk.

"Oh, pshaw!" His mother waved dismissively.

"And speaking of never too late." Phoebe stood. "I believe we're all friends here and I'm tired of hiding. My real name isn't Phoebe Carrie. It's Phoebe Carrington."

"I don't get it," Joe said. "Why would you shorten your last name like that?"

"Shush, Joe. Let her talk." Mom nudged him.

Phoebe had the rapt attention of everyone seated at their family table. Tutti leaned forward, as if worried he'd miss a syllable even though he was only five inches from Phoebe.

"I didn't want you all to think of me differently. When I told Marco, I was worried he would change. But he's been fine. Well, mostly." She tossed her hair back and tipped her chin. "I'm still the person you all met. *Nothing* has changed."

She sat back down to a silence that stretched...and stretched.

"Carrington as in Carrington Tech?" Dylan finally spoke.

"No way," Joe murmured.

"Oh honey, I always thought you looked familiar!" His mother said.

"You *know* me?" Phoebe went hand to heart and Marco felt the tightness in his chest again.

"Everyone knows the Carringtons," Dylan said.

Yeah, not what she'd meant. Marco squeezed Phoebe's hand.

"It's like we have actual royalty in the house!" Tutti clapped.

Rumor was Tutti had stayed up all night to watch the last royal wedding.

"Oh, no. Please. I'm just like anyone else and I want to be treated that way." She turned to Marco. "Right?"

Sure, she was just like everyone else who wore a pearled, sequined wedding gown to slide down a fire escape.

Or curtsied when she met someone. Or shook the hand of every stranger at the bus stop.

If she was like royalty, she was the best of them.

"Tell them, Marco." She elbowed him.

"Sorry. The truth is she's actually *not* like everyone else." All eyes turned to him. "She's better."

CHAPTER 12

"I remember when I saw you for the first time."
~ meme

This was the "found" extended family Phoebe would have had if her mother hadn't died. These were the dinners she should have enjoyed while growing up. There would have been visits with her mother's friends. The house would have been filled with music, art, and amazing food. Mom would have insisted that Daddy have dinner with them every night he was in town and would have never sent Phoebe to a boarding school.

And Marco. Wonderful and charming *Marco*. He was part of this happy and close-knit family she wanted for herself. He seemed comfortable in the midst of the constant chatter and loud laughter.

After dinner, they all gathered outside where white fairy lights were strung from sycamore tree to apple tree. The night was crisp and clear. Their conversations were varied and interesting, from a latest exhibit at the museum, to attending mass on Miracle Sunday, to the latest James Bond movie.

And no one said a *word* about stocks, money, business, or politics.

"When I was a young girl in Spain," Abuelita said in her thick accent, "every man I knew was married by age twenty-five. All my friends ask: 'Pepita, what is *wrong* with your grandsons? Why are they not yet married?' What should I tell them? In my country, you would each have three children by now."

"Mami—" Alice Reyes held up a palm.

"Abuelita, tell your friends Charley and I are getting married in six months." Dylan draped an arm around his fiancée. "It's the earliest Padre Suarez could do it."

"What about you, Marco? Who would marry someone who lives on a boat? Bah! They must think you're a pauper." She grumbled words in Spanish that Phoebe did not understand despite her year studying abroad. "And Joe. Surfing all the time. Why not get married instead?"

"While marriage sounds like a good trade for surfing, I guess I haven't found 'the one.'" Joe held up air quotes.

"Well, look harder!" Abuelita pointed a crooked finger. "Marco?"

"Boy, look at the time," Marco said. "I've got an early morning. Are you ready, Phoebe?"

Grateful to be his ticket out of the questioning, Phoebe took his hand. Good to know the pressure to get married didn't just happen in affluent households. She felt a deeper connection to Marco knowing they'd both been struggling with the same issue in a small way. She was to have settled down with a wealthy man who would take care of her, and apparently Marco was supposed to marry and take care of a woman. They were opposite sides of the same coin.

It took a while to say goodbye to everyone but eventually she and Marco were on the road.

"I think you might like my family better than I do," he said after a few minutes.

"You like them. Don't lie."

"Yeah, they're okay. I guess." The words were said lightly, but he couldn't disguise the tenderness in his voice.

She saw his love clearly in the deep affection he had for both his mother and grandmother, pulling chairs out for them to sit and holding doors open. He did the same for Phoebe, his manners impeccable.

"I hope you don't believe your grandmother. Any woman in their right mind would want to marry you, no matter *where* you live."

"But you think the boat is romantic. I think Abuelita might be right. Having a boat is cool. Living on one is not exactly a chick magnet."

"It's a magnet for this chick." She hooked a finger to her chest.

"Yeah, but let's face it, I'm just an adventure to you."

Phoebe froze, her heart taking the blow. Then anger bubbled up. People always thought of her as the carefree and sweet girl. Always cheerful because she didn't like making trouble or drawing attention to herself. But happiness happened to be a choice she made every morning, and one that didn't always come easily.

"Is that what you think?"

"Isn't it true?"

"No, I'm not having a fun adventure. I'm making the best of my situation, while I try to figure out the rest of my life!"

"Yeah, I know but—"

"No buts!" She held up a palm like he had to her. "Somehow, no matter what I've been through, I give people the impression that my life is filled with unicorns and rainbows."

"Wait. It's not?" He seemed to be fighting a smile.

"*Not* funny!"

"Okay, okay. You don't have to yell."

Oh my gosh, no wonder her vocal cords felt tight and strained. She couldn't remember the last time she'd screamed at anyone. Maybe…never. Well, there was that one time her puppy got loose and headed to a busy street. She'd screamed so loudly that he whimpered and ran back to her, tail between his legs. Her throat ached for a week.

"I *choose* to be happy. It's one of the things I remember best about my mother. Always smiling, enjoying her life. No regrets. Could things be better? Absolutely. Could they also be much worse? Hell, yeah." When they arrived at the marina, she whipped off her seat belt. "But as far as you and the boat go, I would personally live in a *box* with you."

He turned to face her, dark eyes hooded. "Yeah?"

Phoebe had never been one to hold back her affections and tonight would be no exception. When it came to honesty, she gave it freely, even if the favor wasn't always returned. It was a risk every time, and about the only one she ever took before the day she ran out on her wedding.

After Marco had kissed her, after the moment that shook the sense right out of her, she knew whatever they had between them was different. She could no longer pretend he was simply a friend.

"Y-you don't have to tell me that it's crazy because I *know* it is. It doesn't make any sense, but every time you touch me, and when…when we kissed, I feel…please don't laugh…a shimmer and a glow. It's hard to explain."

He simply stared at her, looking stunned, as though she'd taken leave of her senses. "Phoebe, don't—"

"I'm *not* going to stop talking so just…*listen*. I know we didn't kiss at sunset, and I know you don't want me to fall for a myth, but it's happening to me anyway." When he didn't say a word but openly stared, eyes wide, Phoebe gave him her back and reached for the door handle. "You don't have to say anything, and you don't have to feel the same way. But I've never met anyone like you. You're a real hero and not just because of your job, but because you love your family. You went out of your way to help a total stranger. You were kind to me, and I'll *never* forget it. Or you."

She'd just opened the passenger door when she felt Marco's strong arm around her waist, pulling her to him.

"Where do you think you're going?" His deep timbre voice was a low growl as he tugged on her earlobe and sent a swift curl of heat through her. "You can't say something like that and then walk away from me."

"I...wanted to give you time to think."

His laugh was muffled, lips pressed against her neck. Beard stubble tickled, sending tingles down her spine.

"Look, no one understands crazy better than I do. My life is steeped in pandemonium, and chaos follows me wherever I go. But I don't really understand *this*, or what's happening here. Give me a little time to figure it out."

Once, Phoebe's mother had explained that love was never wasted, even when not returned. She'd said that Phoebe had a heart as big as the ocean and would love people and causes all of her life without reservations. Her love wouldn't always be returned but that would have to be okay, too.

Later, her father had told Phoebe she trusted people—mostly men—far too easily and she worried him. She should consider the people she associated with because not everyone had her best interests at heart like he did.

While it didn't make sense, she couldn't disguise this any longer. Her feelings for Marco were deep and fierce. She couldn't deny the pull she had to him. Nor did she want to.

He kissed her, slow and deep, and then when they broke

for air, he took her hand and helped her climb out of his truck.

"C'mere." He tugged her to the boat.

She had no idea what he had in mind but at this point she was all in. Phoebe took his hand, and he helped her aboard. The sun filtered powerful rays of warmth through a thin cloud cover and the seagulls squawked, doing their thing. In the distance, a sailboat could be seen, its sails unfurling, pretty as a picture. Like a movie clip, the first time she'd ever come aboard this boat played. Marco, trying to help, tearing what was left of her wedding dress. The expression on his face as he realized he'd ruined it. Even then she loved him though she couldn't have put those feelings into words.

Maybe all true love happened at first sight.

Marco emerged from where he'd gone below deck, holding a remote of some type. He clicked and suddenly music floated from the speakers, a lovely ballad she recognized. "Starting Over" by Chris Stapleton. On her playlist, too.

He was so lithe and stealthy that before she realized it, Marco had pulled her into his arms. He swung her around the deck, raised his arm to twirl her, and then brought her back. The man could dance. *Really* dance.

"One more thing I didn't know about you. Did you learn how to dance so you could pick up girls?"

"Maybe." He chuckled then whispered softly near her ear. "But this is different."

They danced around the deck, Phoebe somehow managing to keep up with Fred Astaire, Jr. Before long, they'd attracted the attention of nearly everyone on the pier. Fishermen reeling in their catch even paused what they were doing to watch. Delight pulsed through Phoebe and she knew then and there if she ever had a wedding dance, she'd want it to be this song.

From his sailboat, Drew comically clutched his heart and wiped at his eyes. "I might have to give this love thing another try."

"Oh, we've finally inspired him," Phoebe said, her eyes sparkling. "Can I tell you how much I love this?"

Then Marco dipped her, to the cheers of everyone watching.

MARCO HADN'T EXPECTED to attract a small crowd, but if it gave him points with Phoebe, he didn't mind at all. His semi-expertise on the dance floor was a well-guarded secret to everyone on the marina. He preferred them to think of him as the big heavy-footed firefighter who often smelled like smoke and soot. Someone you did not want to mess with.

With Phoebe, though, he found that he'd do just about anything to impress her.

And he had, judging by the surprised look in her eyes as he moved easily around the deck, avoiding benches and anything else that might trip them. Today, he was light on his feet. And a hell of a lot more graceful than the day he'd ripped her wedding dress. Fun times. He whirled her around for three songs before he stopped.

She pulled out of his arms, faced the pier, and bowed. "And that's the end of today's entertainment, folks."

"Encore!" said Drew. "Encore!"

"Sorry, guys." Phoebe waved. "We're going inside now."

"I'm glad you said it and not me." Marco tugged her back down to the cabin and walked into the galley. "It wasn't my intention to have an audience. Notice how they were all men."

"Which happens to be the case most days on the marina. You're such a good dancer, and we make a cute couple. You have to admit."

"Babe, you're cute. I'm tough."

"You're a teddy bear."

"I'm a bear, I'll give you that. You definitely do not want to poke me when I'm finally sleeping after a long shift."

"I'll remember that."

"Although, I will say that if your intent is to get me *up*, there are certain ways that will work better than others." He sent her a slow wicked smile.

"Oh yeah? And what might those ways be?"

Crossing his arms, he pressed his back against the counter, willing himself to keep his hands off Phoebe. Upstairs just a moment ago, he'd wanted to heave her over his shoulder fireman-style, carry her down to the cabin, and throw her on his bed.

Slow. Don't scare her off. He had to move *slow* with Phoebe. And not only because it would be what she understood, what she was accustomed to, but because he was determined to savor every last moment with her. Both before, during, and after.

"Well," he said, studying the ceiling as if thinking it over. "Naked is always a good place to start."

"That's it? Naked?"

He shrugged. "You want my attention? Show up naked."

"Oh, you men. Too simple." She poked him in the ribs. "If I want to wake you up, I'll poke the bear."

He took her hand and pressed a kiss on the inside of her wrist. "Then you might as easily get a growl."

He didn't smile, knowing he wouldn't scare her, but also certain he wanted her to realize he could be deadly serious. It was all fun and games until two people were alone, and naked, and then Marco stopped joking and playing.

And if he did his work right, nobody laughed for a long, long while.

"Do you bite, too?" Her eyes grew dark and luminous, and

she tipped her chin, practically offering him her soft pink neck.

It did catch him by surprise, and it hit him that she wasn't quite the innocent he'd assumed. "I don't bite unless you want me to."

"Maybe a nibble."

"Don't tease." He palmed the nape of her neck because he sensed she wasn't teasing at all.

Instead, she egged him on. Pursued him. There was little sexier to Marco than a woman who asserted herself.

"I don't tease. I know better than to tease you." Then her hands were gliding under his shirt, touching bare skin.

He kissed her again, pressing his weight against her. His mouth was hard and insistent and above all inviting. If she wanted this from him, he was game. Slightly irritated by the shimmering, he found the harder he kissed, the less he noticed. With Phoebe soft and sweet in his arms, her tongue warm and exploring, he slowly lost himself.

"Are you sure about this?" he said on a ragged breath. If she wanted to back out now, this would be the time. Before she killed him.

"I've never been surer about anything in my life."

Any more thoughts flew out the window. Kissing her again, he cupped her ass, lifting her and moving them toward the bedroom. She fell back against the bed, and he followed, covering her body with his own. She rolled on top of him, then pulled her top off, revealing a silky pink bra. He kissed a bare shoulder, sliding the straps of her bra down. When she lowered her panties, he helped toss them to the side.

He lowered his hands to her naked hips, her cool silky skin pressed against his. His own skin seemed to burn hot as the sun, and everything moved in a slow but steady motion.

The boat rocked and swayed, and Marco got to know Phoebe in a whole new kind of way.

CHAPTER 13

"It was love at every sight." ~ meme

A curl of satisfaction rolled through Phoebe so strong and swift that she sucked in a breath. She could almost feel her heart changing. Glowing and shimmering. Pulsing with raw electricity.

And it seemed like the most natural thing in the world to be naked and in the arms of a man she'd just met.

His mouth moved to her neck, the slight scrape of beard stubble leaving a mark. They were both breathing hard, crushing against each other's warm bodies. Marco's kisses were hot and fierce, his hands skillful at eliciting moans of pleasure out of her. His muscular arms around her, a heavy sweetness took over then and Phoebe let go of all inhibitions. She'd been teasing him before, flirting, and curious. But Marco wasn't playing. No more smiles or casual looks. His normally gentle and friendly face took on a hard and fierce look.

And this was the real her, raw and ripe and ready for anything. He brought it out of her, a need she didn't recognize.

They came together in an explosion of heat which rocked her world.

Later, they lay entwined in each other's arms.

"This is by far the best way to christen a boat." Marco kissed her temple, his deep voice low and grumbly. "I've wanted you straddling me again for a while."

She laughed. "We just met a few days ago. How long could it have been?"

He gave her a slow smile. "Probably since later the day we met. And damn, this way was a whole lot better."

"Without the poufy dress between us."

"With *nothing* between us."

She moved to lower her head to his chest and listen to his strong heartbeat. It seemed like she'd known him forever. Coming from someone who didn't sleep with a man until he'd first met her father (bad idea, it turned out) this type of intimacy had never happened before. But she should have trusted her instincts all along. Marco Reyes was the real deal, and it was time to face facts. She'd fallen in love *without* the sunset kiss. Somehow, she'd been gifted with shimmering and glowing and the absolute magnetism Dawn had mentioned. No matter what else, she and Marco had one-third of the triangle and they had this in spades.

"Tell me what it was like for you growing up," Marco said as his fingers played with her hair.

"You really want to hear this?"

"Sure. It sounds like an unusual childhood, at least for someone like me."

She swept her finger across his chest, drawing an invisible line. "My life is divided into two sections: before and after. When someone you love dies, it's so permanent. And the world is suddenly very different. Completely altered. Before my mother died, my life was far more…normal, I guess."

"How do you mean?"

"My mother and father were a beauty-meets-geek romance." She chuckled at the memories. "Oh boy, did I hear stories. They met at a function where my mother was the event coordinator. One of those business showcases where my father was trying to sell his software product to investors. She claims she didn't know much about technology, but she understood people. And because she thought he was so cute in his wire-rimmed glasses, with a strand of long hair that kept falling over one eye, she introduced him to several investors. One of them wound up buying my father's product and he was on his way. His side of the story is that she snuck out like Cinderella at the ball but without leaving a glass slipper. He chased after her, supposedly to thank her, and tried for weeks to track her down. When he finally found her, he didn't give up until she'd have coffee with him. My father didn't have anything when he met my mother. She really loved him."

"I bet he spoiled her once he could."

"Of course, and I can't tell you how many times I heard her tell him that he'd already given her enough. All she wanted was for us to spend time together, which of course got to be less and less once my father's company went public. After a while, my mother and I took trips alone. We could have gone anywhere in the world, but we visited people who had far less than we did. We stayed at her friends' homes in the Bay Area because she wanted me to see that most people didn't have the kind of privileges we did. She didn't want to raise a snob, or someone who took our lifestyle for granted."

He snorted. "Phoebe, you're the furthest thing from a snob I've ever met."

"Then I guess she succeeded."

"How did your mother die?"

"Car accident. One of the rare times she left me behind for a trip. I was twelve. She was driving home from the airport and a meeting she'd had with the head of a foundation she ran."

"I'm sorry, babe." He tugged on a lock of her hair.

"It's all right now. Ever since I met you, I can't help but think that in her final moments she was with somebody like you. Someone kind and good, who might have been with her in her last minutes. She might not have been as frightened. It used to scare me to think she'd been alone, but I know she wasn't. Not really." She tilted her chin to meet his eyes. "You're a hero. You and all the other first responders who work so hard and are always helping."

"Even if we don't always succeed?"

"Yes. Even then." She kissed the tip of his chin. "Now it's your turn to tell me about little Marco. What were you like?"

"My mother used to call me Marco, the patron saint of strays."

"Did you bring every stray dog and cat home?"

"I could never keep any of them. The closest they ever made it was our fenced backyard. Too many of our boarders had allergies. It was safer to leave furry pets outside. Eventually they tunneled under the fence or took advantage of an open one and ran away again. That's why they were in trouble in the first place. Some animals can't change their nature."

"Their nature to run?"

"A lot of these pets had been mistreated and abandoned. Maybe it would have been different if I could have taken them inside the house. I don't know."

Phoebe pictured a young Marco, trying to rescue these poor creatures who ran away again, an image too sweet for words. The fact that he'd think it might have been his fault was rather telling. Phoebe laid her head on his chest, listening to his strong and steady heartbeat.

He caressed her cheek with the back of his hand, which she took in her own and kissed. Then she kissed his neck, making her way to his lips.

They spent the rest of the day in a tangle of sheets and kisses, chuckles and moans. Eventually, they decided to have lunch, so they dressed. But Marco went commando, wearing nothing but his board shorts. She wore nothing but his SFFD tee.

Lunch was a pancetta grilled sandwich with lettuce and tomato on sourdough bread that made Phoebe's toes curl. Again. First, Marco's kisses and his incredible lovemaking skills, and now this.

"Oh my gosh, this is delicious," Phoebe said after taking one bite.

"I call it a PLT."

"I'm calling it my reason to get up in the morning." She took another bite, the pancetta and crusty bread a perfect combination.

He studied her from underneath his eyelashes. "I have to tell you something and you shouldn't get upset."

Her spine stiffened. "Whenever someone tells me I shouldn't get upset, I think I'm going to have a good reason to be upset."

"While I was at the station, I had a visit from a friend of yours."

Everything inside Phoebe stilled. *"Who?"*

"We weren't introduced. But let's just say we recognized each other immediately."

"Ivan."

"That *can't* actually be his name."

"It is."

"Hilarious. Well, Ivan is looking for you and he thought I might know where to find you."

"You covered for me."

Marco wouldn't be intimidated, and that knowledge bathed over her in a soft and sweet warmth.

"I told him that I'd left you at the bus stop which wasn't even a lie."

"Thank you."

Delicious sandwich and all, she left her place setting and climbed into Marco's lap.

"No one's ever taken care of me like this. Marco, thank you. Too many people would just tell him where I was."

"You're welcome." He shifted her on his lap. "You really shouldn't be sitting on me like this, wearing no underwear. It might give me ideas."

"Good." She smiled against his lips. "Tell me something. Are you just an amazing lover or is it our connection?"

"I'd like to claim the skills, but no. It's not always like this." He kissed her and then pulled back to frame her face. "But you know this can't go on forever."

"Already getting tired of me?"

"I don't think I could ever get tired of you, Phoebe Carrington."

The sweet words made her heart twist. "But..."

"You need to fix this rift between you and your father. I was raised to believe family is important. And it sounds like your father loves you. He must have thought he was doing the right thing."

"I know. But it doesn't change the fact he was wrong."

"If you stand up to him, he'll respect you for that. Tell him you're going to make your own choices. Live your own life."

"I will. Promise. That's my plan."

. . .

THOUGH PHOEBE'S days were spent helping others find love, her nights were spent with Marco, anchoring out on the bay for several hours enjoying the views of the skyline. Sailboats fluttered in the distance, the scenery pretty as a postcard.

"Do you want to navigate?" Marco smiled one evening from behind the wheel, cheeks ruddy and windburned.

"You don't have to ask me twice."

He'd positioned her in front of the wheel and stood close behind while she did as he'd taught her, pressed levers, and maneuvered them back to the boat slips. She felt powerful steering as they raced across the waves, cold saltwater spraying her cheeks. Once, she'd spied a dolphin jumping through the waves in the distance and considered it a good omen.

She was no longer thinking about how she'd figure out the rest of her life. This would be her life. Helping others to find the love she'd found.

But after two blissful days, it was time for Marco to go back to firefighting.

After dropping him off at the station, Phoebe drove back to the marina, arriving when Drew was pulling in from his two-day sailing trip around Angel Island. Phoebe stood by and watched him for several minutes. There was something so beautiful and majestic about a sailboat's tall masts.

"How was your trip?"

"Some fishing. Lots of water."

She made a face. "That's it?"

"Honestly, I'm getting sick of boat life. Thinking I might sell *The Fanny*. I'll get top dollar the closer we get to Sunset Kiss Day."

"I've got news for you. A person can fall deeply in love without ever having kissed at sunset."

"Oh, I know. Done that several times myself."

She chuckled. "I thought you enjoyed sailing. And *Fanny*.

What a cute name. How did you come up with it, anyway? Is it an old girlfriend? Sister? Mother?"

"I chose that name because the boat club would probably frown on me christening her with what I like to call my last Mrs. Thanks to her, I came away with my sailboat. Not much else."

"That's terrible. I'm so sorry."

"Don't be. I can be an idiot sometimes. Honestly, I thought living on this sailboat was the answer to being alone. Most women think I have nothing to offer them. They're right in a way."

"I'm sure they're not. You're a good guy and anyone can see that."

"A good guy with some mileage. But seeing you and Marco makes me want to try again. Hell, maybe there's something to this sunset kiss legend. At this point, I'm willing to give it a try."

"That's the spirit!"

Phoebe spent her day off helping Drew spruce up *The Fanny,* now finding the name ironic. She'd changed into worn jeans and a sweatshirt, and on her hands and knees she used a brush to scrub the deck clean.

Because Drew wanted to repay her for helping, he took Phoebe for a short sail around the bay.

As she sat on the boat and watched him work the sails, she marveled at her new life. She didn't miss her old world in the slightest. Eventually, she'd find an apartment so that she and Marco could have a relationship without her being completely dependent on him.

Freedom was the sweetest thing she'd ever tasted.

. . .

Every day moved one more step toward the Sunset Stroll event. Phoebe had spreadsheets she'd organized into a color-coded system.

"I don't know what I ever did without you," Dawn said.

Phoebe had loved being a librarian, organizing, reading stories, and dreaming of her own great love affair. Now, her organizations skills were making her shine in Dawn's eyes, and becoming part of a business that encouraged love, that sought to help others find happiness...well, it was perfect.

"We have a problem." Amanda strolled into Dawn's office, as usual looking like a runway model. While the office of her new franchise was being prepped, she'd been helping with details of the event. "The venue has canceled on us."

Dawn stood. "What? This is an outrage!"

"Why would they do such a thing at the last minute?" Phoebe said.

Amanda winced. "The owner is one of your few match fails."

Dawn face-palmed. "Not the billionaire?"

"Yes," Amanda said.

"He insisted I match him with a much younger woman, thinking his money would make up for the fact that he's a jackass!" Dawn said. "I should have never listened to him."

"Maybe we should be done with these tech moguls," Amanda said. "No one can ever please them."

Phoebe lowered her head and counted the list of entries to the Sunset Stroll event. She'd neglected to mention her association with Ethan and no one had yet made the connection to her father.

Sensing the perfect moment to take the focus off tech moguls, Phoebe piped up. Not long after the family dinner, Charley had texted Phoebe that she hadn't found anyone else to serve and asked for her help.

"I can ask my friend Charley, who owns the Sunrise

Bistro & Bakery in Miracle Bay. She and her fiancé are a sunset kiss couple and would probably love to support the event."

Both Amanda and Dawn stared at Phoebe like she was the answer to a prayer. She wasn't going to lie, it felt great to be this helpful. At the library, no one ever seemed as grateful when she led them to the perfect memoir or latest mystery thriller, or found a book to help them research their family genealogy.

"Would you? That's incredible. I would *much* rather have the event in Miracle Bay," Dawn said.

"I'm seeing her tomorrow night, and I'll ask her then."

CHAPTER 14

"I'm not sure if this is love or a heart arrhythmia." ~ Marco Reyes

"The good thing about tonight is that this is a set menu they've chosen ahead of time," Charley explained. "And they've already paid in advance, but don't worry. They always leave tips and those are all for you. All I need you to do is welcome them, show them to their tables, and remind them of the dishes they've ordered. I've printed some menus. Then, you'll bring each dish out individually. Can you pour wine?"

Phoebe had definitely watched plenty sommeliers in action. How hard could it be?

"Yes, no problem. I've got this." She gave Charley a thumbs-up.

"Okay, well. I certainly don't expect perfection. Thank you so much for doing this. You're a lifesaver!" Charley squeezed Phoebe's shoulders.

"If you don't mind, I'd already like to call in a favor."

"So soon?" Charley crossed her arms and jutted her hip out. "What does Marco want?"

"No, it's not for him."

"Are you sure? You two seemed pretty cozy the other night."

"We are close, at least I like to think so."

"I can assure you I've never seen Marco behave this way around a woman. I knew one day he'd get bitten by the love bug. All right, name the favor. A four-course meal? A special dessert?"

"All of that sounds amazing but I think my favor would be great for your business."

Phoebe went on to explain the Sunset Stroll event, put on by her new employer, the Happy Matchmaker. Not surprisingly, Charley was game.

"As long as you all set up. The place is small, but there's also room outside and we're certainly on a good street for strolling."

When Charley went back in the kitchen, Phoebe busied herself by perusing the menu. The appetizers were a spinach and feta tarte soleil, and broccoli and garlic ricotta toasts with hot honey. The entrée, quail legs with tamarin glaze and fig chutney. Dessert? Tofu mango mousse pudding.

A gourmet meal worthy of her failed wedding reception. Ethan had hired a five-star Michelin chef from New York City for their sit-down dinner. Their main course was to have been coffee-marinated mutton chops in a balsamic reduction sauce. Phoebe loved coffee but marinating a mutton chop in it seemed like a waste of beans. Not that anyone had asked her. Aunt Sarah had chosen everything down to the smallest detail. Even the wedding dress. The worst thing was that Phoebe had allowed it.

She busied herself setting the tables and noticed with a

bit of rearranging, they could get more chairs and tables in here for the event.

Phoebe retrieved the white linen tablecloths from a plastic bin in the back and draped each table with their cloth. Then she arranged the place settings along with single tapered candles as centerpieces. But the napkins weren't going easily into their swan shapes. Phoebe googled "how to make a swan napkin" and propped her phone on the centerpiece to watch the video tutorial.

Fold, fold. Point. Fold. Point. Define creases. Fold again. But *her* swan appeared to have a broken neck. She tried again and again, finally arriving at something passable.

"Can I do anything else to help?" Phoebe peeked in the back where Charley was plating dishes.

"I've got this. Just stand by the door and welcome our guests. And remember, the customer is always right."

Phoebe smoothed hands down her creased black slacks. She hadn't been told how to dress, but Phoebe wanted to make a good impression. She'd worn classic black and a white button-down blouse. Hair pulled back from her face in a high ponytail, she believed she'd nailed the look of "waiter at high-end restaurant." She resolved to be attentive to her guests, thankful this wasn't exactly a trial by fire. They had only six guests in total but, according to Marco, these people paid ridiculous amounts of money for Charley's food.

They'd probably also expect the kind of top-notch service to match. On her last dinner with Ethan, days before the wedding, he'd berated a waiter for not bringing dessert quickly enough.

"Couldn't you be kinder? He's doing the best he can."

"I tip them generously, and for that I deserve top quality service."

"Well, it's not like he can materialize the crème brûlée. I

believe he has to get it from the kitchen. Maybe it's the *chef* who's overwhelmed."

"Excuses, excuses. Phoebe, I haven't reached the top of the high-tech world with rationalizations for this or that."

You mean you haven't managed a business monopoly by making excuses.

"Everybody has a story. You could be a little kinder to those less fortunate."

"I'm *generous,*" he said, as if that replaced compassion.

Phoebe now believed that was the moment she'd decided she couldn't go through with the wedding. But her father, Aunt Sarah, and Flannery had formed a three-prong attack to talk Phoebe right back into making the biggest mistake of her life.

"You're the best thing that could ever happen to a man like Ethan Bellamy," her father had said. "Your kindness will rub off on him."

"You'll change him for the better," Flannery agreed.

Obviously, Phoebe disagreed.

Now, a middle-aged couple approached the bistro, the man holding the door open for his female companion.

"Welcome." Phoebe curtsied when they entered, then remembered that was probably inappropriate. "I'm Phoebe, your server."

She was awkward all over again, hands folded in front of her. But this seemed too subservient and she wanted these people to realize servers were as worthy as anyone else.

With a flourish of her hand, she led them to their table. "Welcome to Charley's Bistro."

"I thought it was Sunrise Bistro?" the woman asked.

"Oh, you're right. Sorry, I'm new here."

"We've been on the wait list for weeks." The man unfolded the lame swan and draped it across his lap. "Looking forward to this."

"We're excited to have you. These are your menus." Phoebe indicated to the slips of embossed paper on the tables. "Do you enjoy gourmet cuisine?"

"Why, yes." The man reached for the woman's hand. "My wife and I both do. Particularly French cuisine, but tonight we decided to try this."

"Did you know that the most popular alcoholic drink in France is Calvados, an apple brandy made in Normandy?" Sometimes having once been a librarian with plenty of free time on her hands paid off.

The man smiled, leaning back in his chair. "Why yes. Have you tried it?"

"Only once."

Remembering Ethan thought it a great quality when a waiter could disappear at the right time, Phoebe excused herself after bringing them goblets of iced water.

In the back, she found Charley pulling trays from the oven.

"The other guests aren't here yet," Phoebe said. "Should I start serving the couple that's arrived?"

She pointed to the plated dishes lined up on the side. "Go ahead. We always have someone who's fashionably late."

The husband and wife were enjoying the spinach and feta tarts when a group of men approached, ambling together down the sidewalk like a school of fish. More like sharks, actually, but they were solitary creatures. The business suits were familiar, the cigar one of them brandished classic for a celebratory dinner. Maybe another chance to be joyous over a competitor's demise. Tonight, she'd smile if it killed her.

"Welcome." Phoebe remembered not to curtsy this time. "This way, please."

She led the four gentlemen to their table and pointed to the menus. "These are your courses."

Three took their seats, but one man continued to stand and openly stared. "*Phoebe?* It's me, Edward Cahalan."

Oh no. His silver shark suit, um, silver double-breasted suit was familiar. She wasn't sure how she knew him, or even if she did, but he definitely knew her.

Asking for God's forgiveness in advance, she faked an English accent. "No, sorry. Y-you must have me confused with someone else," she lied. "My name is…Jane. Jane Austen."

She was going to guess none of these men had ever read *Pride & Prejudice* or any other of her classics.

"My *God*! You look just like Phoebe Carrington!"

"Don't be ridiculous," one of the men said. "What would Phoebe be doing *here* of all places?"

"She's been hospitalized for extreme exhaustion," the other man said. "You heard Bellamy."

"We all know that's another word for rehab," the fourth man said, perusing the menu.

Phoebe gasped.

"Don't sound so shocked," Ed said to her. "It's the disease of the affluent."

Phoebe let that sit with her for a moment. She'd never even smoked marijuana, which Flannery had assured her was perfectly legal now.

"She's as spoiled as they come." Ed sat. "Might we get our appetizers sometime today?"

"We have a reservation for *six*." One man held up his Rolex.

Never mind that they'd waltzed in *fifteen* minutes late.

"I'm quite sorry, sir. Coming right up."

But the nice couple were done with their first appetizer. Phoebe made three trips bringing out their next appetizer, catching an exchange of sweet words of endearment from the couple. Then she brought the men's appetizers, listening to them grumble about the Dow Jones.

"Miss? We ordered a bottle of Cabernet Sauvignon. Might we have it now?" the husband asked nicely.

"Oh, quite sure, sir. I'll be right with you." Thank goodness for her addiction to British baking shows. Her accent was impeccable.

In the kitchen, Charley was muttering away. Something about aged cheese. Phoebe found the bottle, corkscrew right next to it. Perfect! She carried both over to the couple's table and set the bottle down.

The corkscrew was different than the ones she'd seen used before, but it was simple enough to figure out that the screw should go in the cork. Hence, the term corkscrew. By George, she had this! She began twisting the screw, winding it further and further down until she felt it must have reached New Zealand. As she did, two metal prongs gradually rose on either side. This must mean something.

The husband's eyes were wide with amazement because she was obviously the best he'd ever seen at this. Maybe she should consider becoming a sommelier since this was such fun. Still, she couldn't figure out the last part even after jiggling the bottle a few times.

"I think you're supposed to do it like *this*," the husband said slowly, pressing down on the levers that were stuck out to the side.

Phoebe had been afraid that would break something, but instead the cork rose to the surface and easily popped off.

"Right-o. That's the way you do it!" She then poured expertly into their glasses.

"I'm sorry, did you just develop an English accent?" the husband said, squinting.

"Um..."

"Jane, we're ready for our next course," Rehab Man barked.

"*Jane?* I thought you said your name was Phoebe," the wife said.

"It is. It's Jane Phoebe." She cleared her throat. "Excuse me."

She brought one entrée after another for the businessmen, and each time she got a scowl and a wrinkled nose. Apparently, she wasn't fast enough. There went her tip, she guessed, not that she'd counted on much from them in that department.

With everyone eating, drinking, or chatting, Phoebe took five. She leaned against the back wall of the restroom and tried to breathe. Silently she blessed every service worker in America and, in fact, the entire world. The pressure to perform was killing her. She wet a paper towel and put it to her forehead. Her worst days at the library hadn't even come a smidgen close to this. Even now, dealing with the queen of disorganization at Happy Matchmaker was nothing compared to this fresh hell.

Then she remembered the kind of waiter that her mother used to love. Someone who told stories and entertained the customers. Once, on a trip to Africa with her parents, they'd been told about safaris like the kind that Ernest Hemingway wrote about. Stories of lions and tigers and elephants that had a young girl enthralled.

Toning down the English accent, she went back to the wife and husband. "Are you enjoying your dinner?"

"Very much," the wife said. "Our compliments to the chef."

"Indeed." The husband raised his wine.

"She'll be out shortly," Phoebe said. "For now, may I tell you a little bit about Miracle Bay?"

"What's that?" the husband asked.

"The nickname for this neighborhood, honey." The wife reached for her husband's hand. "Remember? I told you."

Phoebe had her customers' rapt attention as she told the story of the original sunset kiss lovers starring Celeste and Hugo Ortiz. By the time she neared the end of their love story, the wife's eyes were watery.

"We've been married thirty years. True love." She wiped her eyes.

"Did you…see him shimmer when you first met him?" Phoebe asked.

The wife wrinkled her nose. *"Shimmer?"*

"Some people think that's what happens with love at first sight."

"It wasn't love at first sight," the man said with a chuckle. "She *hated* me at first sight."

"Sometimes it takes a second look." The wife winked.

Phoebe couldn't imagine hating Marco. Then again, he'd saved her by breaking her fall. But yikes, the whole brawny firefighter thing and smoldering dark looks would have won her over anyway.

"Excuse me. I'm going to go check on your dessert."

"Poor Carrington," Ed said. "No one would have seen this coming."

"You can't fault him," Rehab Man said. "It could happen to any one of us."

"It's been going on for months. David should have been better prepared. Now he could lose everything."

"Keep your friends close and your enemies closer," Ed muttered. "He started that company with his wife. It's not right to ask him to resign."

Phoebe strained to hear more. Was her father in trouble? Why hadn't he told her? Then again, she understood how rumors got started. Usually by a person's competitor. It couldn't be true. It just couldn't be.

Charley bustled out, wearing her chef's hat and apron. She greeted the couple first. "I hope you've enjoyed your meal tonight."

Charley didn't bow or curtsy. She didn't appear subservient *or* superior. She was fully in charge of herself and Phoebe envied her. Someday she'd have the natural confidence Charley exuded.

"It's all been wonderful," the wife gushed. "And hearing all about the legend of the sunset kiss was such a bonus."

"Oh, yes. This is a very special area," Charley said. "If you're ever in the neighborhood on a Sunday, we have donuts half price. We call it Miracle Sunday around here."

"You serve donuts, too?"

"That's how we started out. Sunrise Bakery owned and operated by my foster mother, Coral Monroe. My sister Milly and I grew up working in the shop. Baking was my first love."

Charley briefly spoke to the businessmen who honestly didn't seem to want to talk to her anyway. They finally filed out, leaving a measly tip probably worth .0001 percent of their net worth.

"Fascists," Phoebe muttered, picking up the bills. Better than nothing.

Since Charley was occupied with the wife and husband, telling them all about her and Dylan's "accidental" kiss, Phoebe stepped outside. She pulled out her cell and dialed.

He picked up immediately. "Phoebe."

"Hi, Daddy."

"How are you, Pumpkin?"

The resignation in her father's words made Phoebe's heart ache. "I'm…really sorry."

"Come home, and we'll talk about it."

"I didn't want to marry Ethan, and I told you. You wouldn't listen."

Silence on the other end.

"I'm going to pay you back for the wedding. Every penny. I'll use all of my savings."

"I didn't pay for the wedding. Ethan did."

She owed *Ethan* money and not her father. But asking the groom to pay for a wedding wasn't traditional and her father would have paid for everything unless…these rumors were true.

"Daddy, are you…are you in trouble?"

He sighed. "Nothing for you to worry about."

"I'm twenty-nine not twelve. You would have talked to Mom about this. She was your partner. You can talk to me, too."

"You're not my partner, Phoebe, you're my daughter. It's always been my job to take care of you and this is beyond your understanding. You've always hated any talk about business. Your mother did, too, but she had at least a working knowledge."

Phoebe scoffed. "Dumb it down for me, then."

"I'm sorry. I didn't mean to imply you lack intelligence. Far from it. Just a lack of inclination."

"You're not wrong. Now, explain."

"There have been a few changes recently that took our company by surprise. We didn't act quickly enough and lost market share." He paused for a beat. "It's not looking good for bouncing back. I'm going to be asked to step down as CEO."

"Of your own *company*?"

"We have a board like every other publicly traded company, and they've been unhappy for months."

"But Daddy, you and Mom started that company!"

"The company she helped me start is eons away from what exists now."

"Why didn't you tell me about any of this?"

"Aunt Sarah believed I shouldn't worry you. She suggested a marriage to Ethan would at least take care of your future. Even if I lose everything and have to start over, you'll be taken care of. He's been interested in you for a long time."

Ethan had been interested in her for a long time. How long? She was only twenty-nine for crying out loud. Ew.

"You shouldn't have *listened* to Aunt Sarah."

"I'm beginning to realize that."

"All I've ever wanted was your respect. You can only see me as an extension of yourself, but I'm a person with my own ideas."

"It's my fault, I know, but you're not prepared to be self-sufficient. When you wanted to study English Literature, I said, why not? Sarah thought you should follow me into business and eventually be my right-hand man. I knew you'd never be happy. I tried to do what your mother would have done. But as you've probably discovered by now, it's tough to make a living doing what you love. I happened to be one of the lucky ones. There's actual money in what I do."

Thinking of her silly dream to be paid to read, Phoebe cringed. It was true that she'd been far too sheltered. Ignorant of real struggles. Tonight, she'd discovered how hard some people worked to survive. It was humbling.

"I can't believe you wanted me to marry Ethan so I'd be taken care of for the rest of my life. I don't care what happens to me. What about *you*?"

"I've been poor before just like your mother, but, Pumpkin, you never have. And I don't think you should have to start now."

"If walking away from a church full of people didn't tell you anything, then you're not listening. I don't want that life. The only advantage I've ever seen with having plenty of money is being able to help others."

"And that's not a small thing."

He was right.

"We should have this conversation in person. I'm coming by tomorrow to pick up my car."

"I honestly don't know how you've managed without one. You're more resourceful than I've given you credit."

"See? I'm already surprising you."

CHAPTER 15

"True love stories never have endings." ~ meme

The next day, Phoebe drove Marco's truck to the station. She'd hoped to see him, and let him know of her plan, but according to the dispatcher, the guys were out on a call. And anyway, she would be back long before his shift was at an end. She, however, wanted him to have his truck at the station should he need it. It was also important for him to realize her gradual independence from him and all the help he'd provided. She'd relied on him a little too much, due to her circumstances. But especially now that they were in a relationship, she wouldn't be dead weight. Rummaging through her purse, she found a pen, then dug through Marco's glove compartment searching for a piece of paper, a receipt, anything. She found a box of unopened condoms.

Well, okay. He had those on the boat as well. Who could fault a red-blooded man for always being prepared? It had worked out rather nicely for her.

Eventually she found an old receipt from Sunrise Bakery. But it already had writing on the back: Veronica's phone number in lovely scripted handwriting. A little heart over the "i." The date of the receipt was two months ago. *Yes, she checked.* So, to recap: the love of her life had been around the block a few times. Thanks to Veronica, Phoebe already knew this. It didn't bother her. Much. She'd made mistakes, too. Now everything had changed. They were both done with the past and anyone in it because they'd found each other. He was finished with his commitment-phobia ways.

Phoebe scribbled her note on a napkin and placed it on the dashboard:

I went to pick up my car. I'll probably be back by the time you read this note.

Love,

Phoebe

xoxoxo

She put the keys in the glove compartment and left the truck unlocked. When he got back from the call, he'd probably notice it parked.

This game was over. Phoebe couldn't hide anymore. Not in Miracle Bay and not in New York City. She'd go home and face her father and Aunt Sarah. Running had solved only a temporary problem: her wedding day to Ethan Bellamy. Mission accomplished there, but she had more work to do. Remembering Flannery's words, *I'd believe that if you'd tell Uncle David to his face,* Phoebe decided it was time to do just that. Starting her new life meant saying goodbye to the old one, not running from it.

For the second time in her life, Phoebe used the app on her phone to order a car. This time, she knew exactly how to do it. But when the driver pulled up to the closed iron gates of her family home over an hour away, he turned around to face her.

"Are you *sure* this is where you live?"

"Just punch in the code." She recited the numbers.

The driver tried, twice, but the numbers didn't work. "I hope this isn't some kind of a joke. These people don't take kindly to intruders."

These people. She was related to these people and security must have changed the code. The last time Phoebe had used it was shortly before her non-wedding day.

"It's okay. You can go."

Once the driver left, Phoebe stood in front of the gate and the surveillance camera where she would best be seen. Her father had his share of enemies, hence the security. But it was an odd feeling to be on the outside looking in. She pressed the button to ring the bell, waved, and waited. Waved again.

Slowly, the gates swung open and Phoebe walked up the long circular driveway.

Aunt Sarah met her at the door. "Phoebe, darling."

"Is my father here?"

"They called a last-minute board meeting, so no, he's not." She waved Phoebe inside.

"I just came by to pick up my car and say hello to Daddy. We need to talk."

"Oh honey, I'm sure he'll forgive all. And when will you be moving in the rest of your things? I know you gave up your apartment. I'm assuming since the marriage to Ethan is kaput, you'll be moving back in with David."

"No, I'll be on my own in the city."

"Alone?" Aunt Sarah pursed her lips. "Without a job?"

"I'm working, here and there." She'd made three figures in tips last night, thanks mostly to the generosity of the husband-and-wife couple. They'd enjoyed her stories and hoped to come again. Her first paycheck from the matchmaking job would come in another week, and the work she did there honestly didn't feel like work.

"I'm looking for an apartment."

Granted, all the ads she'd seen were out of her price range, but finding a roommate was her next step.

Phoebe followed Aunt Sarah into the living room. "You're *such* a foolish girl."

Phoebe had been prepared for this from Aunt Sarah, who'd lived well among the Silicon Valley elite, thanks to the generosity of David and Becky Carrington.

"Your father might lose everything, and you could at least help yourself."

Phoebe heard: *"I'm about to lose my free ride and you could help me."*

"Sure. But not by marrying Ethan."

"What can *you* do to help the situation? Have you suddenly grown a PhD in business management? Software development? What do you know about their world? No more than I do, except that you grew up in it." Aunt Sarah walked straight to the built-in bar and filled two glasses with ice.

Phoebe held up a palm. "My father is a genius and even if he loses this company, he'll build another. And probably be begged to return to this one someday if it manages to survive without him."

Phoebe had done her research. After getting back from Charley's, she'd spent the rest of the night doing her due diligence. Men like her father bounced back from losses like this one, and yes, she felt horrible for him, but the cost of her soul was far too expensive. Besides, marrying him would have really only helped Phoebe, and not…

"Oh my God, *you* wanted me to marry Ethan so you could continue to be part of the 'in' crowd! So you could still be invited to the swanky parties and vacations. The wedding was just the beginning."

"Don't be ridiculous."

"Daddy *told* me it was your idea. Don't lie to me."

"I was only thinking of you. Your mother, God rest her soul, spoiled you rotten. She made you believe that good things happen to good people. That's *far* from the truth. Some decent people scrape and work and barely manage to survive."

Phoebe had no doubt this was unfortunately true. Maybe her mother did have an overly optimistic view of the world. But Phoebe would much rather scrape and work hard all of her life than get in bed with the devil. She'd much rather love a man's heart and soul than his wallet. She'd run out of that church like her butt was on fire and if that didn't state her feelings clearly enough, she didn't know what else could.

"I'm sorry you had it tough growing up," Phoebe said. "That tends to color a person's view of the world. I know I must sound ungrateful to you, and I know how privileged I've been. I get it now, believe me. But if Daddy loses everything, then so should I. And it's okay because we still have each other. I hope one day you'll feel that way about someone."

Aunt Sarah scoffed. "You know what? I did once, and then he found a younger model and traded me in."

"I didn't know. I'm sorry."

"I was much younger when we married, of course, and *much* prettier. And thinner."

Poor Aunt Sarah. Phoebe considered telling her about the matchmaking event, but Aunt Sarah seemed far too jaded to have an open heart. Maybe the Sunset Kiss would be better for her.

"Then I suppose it's all the more important for me to find the *right* person while I'm still young. If I could be so lucky."

Like my mother was. Because like Phoebe, and everyone else on earth, Marco would someday grow old, too, and lose his movie-star good looks.

But he'd always have the same kind heart.

"You want to know something funny? You and I are both at fault in a way. I thought I was doing what my mother would want, too, marrying Ethan. She married into the tech world and I figured she'd want that for me. I was trying to be a good daughter. But I'd forgotten something. She loved Daddy when he had nothing. That's who I want to be. The kind of woman who loves a man for who he is."

"Lord, what I wouldn't do to be twenty years younger with such incurable optimism." Aunt Sarah sashayed out of the living room carrying her drink, the ice cubes clinking.

"All you have to do is try," Phoebe called after her.

ALONE, Phoebe eventually fell asleep on the couch waiting for her father. Sitting up at the sound of the front door closing, she rubbed her eyes.

Daddy sat beside her. "Hey, Pumpkin."

"What happened?" She glimpsed at the clock. Midnight. Did they hold board meetings this late?

"Emergency board meeting."

The lines around his eyes were much deeper than she remembered. No words were necessary.

He'd been forced to step down as CEO. Phoebe's throat was tight, and suddenly parched.

"Daddy? Is it going to be okay?"

"It will be okay in the end. And if it's not okay then it isn't the end." He parroted her mother's favorite saying after a business loss. "God, I miss her. Every day."

"Me too." She leaned against his shoulder. "I feel like she'd know what to do right now."

"She probably would, but even if there was nothing to do, the most important thing is that she'd be right here with me."

"You really loved her. I always knew."

"More than anything else in the world. From the moment I laid eyes on her, I was a goner." He cleared his throat. "And I'm sorry if even for one second I suggested you settle for less. She would have taken me to task over it."

"She'd have given you hell, for sure." Phoebe softened her words. "All I've ever wanted for myself was what you and Mom had together. For a while, I was really angry with you for not listening to my doubts about Ethan. For allowing me to be talked into this because you know I've always wanted to be the good daughter. I was almost willing to sacrifice my own happiness for my family's approval. But you should have told me that you were in trouble. You should have told me about Aunt Sarah's plan."

"Would you have gone along with it?"

"No," she admitted. "But I wouldn't have had to wonder whether you really didn't care about my happiness."

"Pumpkin, I do care."

"I realize you did this all out of love. Mom would also understand you were trying to take care of me. If she were here, maybe none of this would have happened. Maybe you wouldn't have lost your company."

"Well, I didn't exactly come out of this situation a poor man. But I started this company with your mother at my side and losing that dream…that's what hurts."

"You don't have to worry about me."

He patted her knee. "I should have had more faith in you. For that, I'm sorry. You haven't even made a single charge on the joint credit card. You're really doing this on your own."

"Not exactly on my own." She sucked in a breath. "I met someone and fell in love."

"Already?" Daddy sat up straighter.

She quirked a brow. "It happened just like it did for you and Mom. From the moment we met."

"Phoebe, I hope this isn't another mistake. Not someone who sees you as a target."

"He didn't even know who I was in the beginning and I faked my last name. His name is Marco Reyes, and he's from a wonderful family."

"Okay, he's from a good family. What does he do for a living?"

"He's a firefighter studying for the lieutenant exam. I know he'll pass it, too, he's so smart. And he's cautious. A lot like…you."

Daddy slowly shook his head but if she wasn't mistaken, he fought a smile. "When am *I* going to meet him?"

"Don't worry, you will. But I don't require your approval. I just…know. Okay?"

"And does he feel the same way?"

"I think so. Yes, he does."

He hadn't said so in so many words, but she saw it in his eyes. Felt the tenderness in their lovemaking. It wasn't just sex between them but so much more. A real and lasting connection.

"If he loves you the way I loved your mother, this is a once in a lifetime kind of thing."

"Maybe so, but I sometimes think you should start dating again."

"Nah, not now. Bad timing. I'm going to be busy building a new company from the ground up. Starting over."

"Make room for love, Daddy. Mom would have wanted that for you."

He ignored that statement, stood, and pulled her to her feet. "I assume you're staying the night since you waited for me."

"Sure, I'll stay. And maybe we can have breakfast in the morning with Aunt Sarah. Just like old times. But you should know I'm going back. Neither one of you are going to talk me into staying."

"I wouldn't dream of it." He faced her. "But before you go back, make time to speak to Ethan. It's the right thing to do."

"Of course. I owe him a lot of money, apparently." She sighed. "I'll pay him back one way or another."

"It's a drop in the bucket to him. He's the one who wanted all the pomp and circumstance. He thought he was marrying royalty in a way. My daughter, which was a coup for him."

"I was going to do it all for you, Daddy. You and Mom both because I thought she would have wanted me to. Until I remembered she loved you when you had nothing."

"That's true. She helped me. We helped each other. But it wasn't always easy."

"I'll be ready for some tough times to come. And I won't give up."

"If you fell in love that quickly, chances are there's a lot you don't know about him yet."

Phoebe heard a difference in the way her father spoke now. She didn't hear manipulation this time, but only concern. It sounded as though he were speaking to his equal, and pride rushed through her.

"You're right. I'll get to know him better, but even though I know he won't be perfect, I can't say I'll ever stop loving him."

PHOEBE SPENT the night at her father's and in the morning thought of texting Marco to see if he'd noticed the truck. Even if it was parked behind the station in a protected area, she didn't want anyone else finding the key in the glove compartment. But he'd probably already seen the truck and read her note. If he had any questions, he'd text her. Marco was a secure and confident man, and it was a good feeling to know at least *he* had faith in her and had from the beginning.

The next morning, she wandered down for breakfast in the dining room. She found Aunt Sarah, sipping her coffee.

"Good morning."

"I only stayed the night because it was late when Daddy got home. Is he joining us?"

"You just missed him. I believe he'll be in meetings with bankers and financiers all day. Restructuring, that kind of thing." She shook her head. "I've no idea what it involves."

Phoebe reached for the coffee carafe.

"Jenna can make you a mocha latte if you prefer," Aunt Sarah said, speaking of the live-in housekeeper and cook.

"No, this is fine." She poured coffee into the cup printed with silver and gold leaves and stirred in sugar from the sterling silver dispenser.

How had she never before noticed the clinical sparseness of the dining room? They'd moved into this house after her mother's death because Daddy couldn't stand to be around all the memories of her in the first house they'd ever owned. That had been less of a mansion and more of a large family home, but Aunt Sarah had helped Daddy find this home. She'd been given free rein to decorate their home since he didn't care about that sort of thing. He occasionally hosted business dinners here, though, which probably made their kitchen less like home and more like a high-end restaurant.

In Mrs. Reyes's boardinghouse every piece of furniture and dish was secondhand, mismatched, and…cozy. They were also bright and colorful. No matter who they were or where they came from, Alice managed to make everyone who lived with her feel at home. Phoebe thought of Tutti and Abuelita and all the boarders that made that big house a home. When Marco got home from his shift, she'd suggest that they go to dinner with his family again.

"Aunt Sarah," Phoebe said. "I'm sorry I rushed out of the church without telling you. I was worried you'd try to talk me out of leaving. And…and I *had* to leave. Please understand."

"I apologize that I made you feel you couldn't come to me with your concerns. Your worries."

"Maybe while I'm here, I should try to talk to Ethan. Do you know if he's back from China yet?"

The doorbell rang just as Aunt Sarah opened her mouth, then closed it.

Phoebe was not too surprised to find Ethan in the dining room a few seconds later.

"I guess I read your mind," Aunt Sarah said, standing. "I knew you'd want to see him."

Phoebe briefly studied the place setting to avoid having to look directly at him. "I thought you were in China."

"Quick trip." He did not sit, his moves abrupt and impersonal. "Do you want to do this here, or out on the patio?"

"Um, on the patio." She led the way, trying not to give him a second glance.

Though she should have been prepared for this, it had been tough enough to get through the talk with her father. She hadn't looked forward to Ethan, and this was before she'd found out *he* paid for their wedding. It would have been nice to have a break between the two. A chance to regroup. Ethan always managed to terrify her. As usual his scent was a combination of designer cologne and cigar smoke. He dressed in his standard gray double-breasted suit and red power tie, as if he went everywhere ready to attend a board meeting.

Once they were both out on the stone patio, he shut the sliders and turned to her with a glare. "What do you have to say for yourself, young lady?"

"I'm sorry."

"You certainly are. Why did you walk out on me? Didn't I give you everything a woman could want?"

"Actually, it was more like you gave my Aunt Sarah everything *she* wanted in a wedding. I happened to be along for the ride."

Ethan shook his head slowly. "No one walks out on me, Phoebe. I don't care who your father is."

"I...I don't know what more I can say to you. We were a horrible match from the start. You don't love me because you don't even *know* me. I never wanted to quit my job and you asked me to. That's really quite inconsiderate if you want to know the truth." She tipped her chin.

"*Inconsiderate?* Phoebe, you're a *librarian*." He snorted. "And do you have any idea how many women would kill to be in your position?"

"Then it shouldn't be that hard to find my replacement."

"You're absolutely right and it won't be."

"I'll pay you back for everything you spent on the wedding."

He scoffed. "It will take you the rest of your life to do that. You don't have that kind of money and pretty soon your father might not, either."

A cold shiver slid down Phoebe's spine. This sounded like a veiled threat. "My father will be fine, and you will not punish him for this in any way."

Ethan tipped back on his heels. "Here's what's going to happen. We've already issued a statement that you've been hospitalized for exhaustion. The wedding has been delayed."

"Forever," Phoebe said. "It's been delayed *forever*."

"I'll need you to issue a statement to the press that after your hospitalization for extreme stress and due to your concern over your father's business, the wedding is off indefinitely."

"Forever, you mean."

He waved a hand dismissively. "Eventually, after a few months have passed, I'll announce my engagement to someone new. No one will even remember you."

"I'll issue my statement, but it won't be a lie. I *wasn't* hospitalized for exhaustion and I'm not going to say I was."

"Why, you little—"

"Ethan." The firm voice belonged to Aunt Sarah, who'd opened the slider door. "I did not ask you here so you could yell at my niece and threaten her. If I were you, I'd leave here now before I do something I regret. Now, she already said she's sorry, and I do believe there's nothing left to say."

"You Carringtons are all alike," he said with disgust, moving toward the exit. "I'll be in touch with a bill for the wedding."

"Try again, Ethan." Aunt Sarah crossed her arms. "You forget that I happen to know you didn't pay a penny. Everything, including that amazing dress, was donated for the publicity involved with being part of the wedding of the year. You and your business manager arranged it that way, because God forbid you actually pay for anything."

Aunt Sarah said the last words to Ethan's back as he slammed the door.

"And by the way, I loved being a librarian!" Phoebe yelled after him.

Her aunt had done the right thing and supported her family. She really did love her brother, and coming to live with them might have truly been about *helping*.

See the best in people, honey. Everyone has at least one redeeming quality and you'll find it if you look carefully enough.

Phoebe had nevertheless failed to do this with Aunt Sarah. No longer.

Aunt Sarah shook with anger. "I didn't know what kind of man he was, or I would have never been okay with your marriage. Please believe that."

The truth was in her aunt's eyes. They were watery and soft with regret.

"Thank you," Phoebe whispered. "How long have you known about the wedding vendors?"

"Not long. But after you were gone, some came to me, upset that they hadn't been paid. And now, they would also not get any publicity. I referred them to Ethan, adding that I felt they should be paid for their work. Obviously, I didn't want you to know because you'd only feel worse."

Yes, she did feel worse. Regret pierced through her skin like a knife, leaving nothing but a dull and throbbing ache.

"One wedding affected so many people."

One choice had hurt people she never intended.

"A wedding should only concern the two people getting married, but that's never the case. Family is always at the center of two people joining together. And of course, in this high-tech world you and I both live in, everything is made far more complicated thanks to all that money."

This was true. Without the support of a family, a marriage would have trouble during the rough spots. She remembered Amanda and Noah's sad love story. Phoebe didn't want complicated.

"Is it so wrong to want simple?"

"It's not wrong," Aunt Sarah said. "Maybe naïve. But never wrong."

CHAPTER 16

"Love is friendship that has caught on fire." ~ meme

"Go fish," said Smitty.

Marco, Smitty, Tony, Johnny, and Dylan were sitting around the card table wearing their helmets and full turn-out gear, counting the minutes until they got another call. Considering the night was young, it could happen at any moment. They'd already had a full day involving a structural fire, for which they'd had to spend hours afterward cleaning equipment. Next, a car accident. The chief had told Johnny to pick up all the big pieces of the wrecked car and give them to the tow truck driver so he could glue them back on the car when he fixed it.

Yep, Johnny believed him, and did as told. The rest of them couldn't stop laughing.

But even with comic relief, they had no doubt they weren't done tonight. First, there was a full moon. Secondly,

Marco was still on shift. Third, there was a Giants game going on, which always meant a call to someone passed out on the bleachers drunk and possibly requiring medical attention. In other words, the deck was stacked against them.

Tony grabbed a few cards out of the pile and set one down.

"Do you have any nines?" Dylan said with a long-suffering sigh.

"Go fish," said Marco.

"This is boring," said Johnny, flipping through his cards.

"Any minute now," said Smitty. "Keep your helmet on."

"We should be playing poker," said Marco.

"Poker is too involved," said Tony. "I like to set up my strategy and this game requires zero thinking."

But a few hours later, with no calls, Marco began to relax along with the rest of them. Helmets were removed, turn-out gear pulled off. And Marco did something he hadn't thought he would for quite a while. He searched for an apartment to rent. Something good enough for a woman like Phoebe, but still affordable on a public servant's salary. He nearly bit his tongue off at the prices of rentals in decent parts of the city. There was no way he'd swing this until he passed the lieutenant exam and, even then, it would be tough.

He'd always lived with roommates, and with Dylan for a while in the restored Victorian he'd planned to flip but decided to keep. At one time, Dylan had flipped houses with a partner, and Marco sometimes helped with the handiwork. Though Dylan was only doing the occasional house flip now, he still had connections. Every ten years or so, a deal came up in the city. Someone was down on his luck and had to sell quickly. Maybe Marco could put in the sweat equity and find something he could live with.

He told himself he was only killing time when he asked Dylan if he had any leads on future house flips.

"Why? Tired of living on a boat?"

"Maybe."

"Does this have anything to do with Phoebe?"

"Why do you ask that?"

"Because you said the boat made the perfect bachelor pad, and I wonder if that's changed. Has it?"

Marco fought a smile. "Yeah. I guess she's pretty...amazing."

"Ironic that you literally had to be hit over the head with love." Dylan laughed, having himself a great old time at Marco's expense.

"Are you having fun?"

"Actually, yes." Dylan stood and clapped Marco's shoulder. "I'll get in touch with some of my contacts and see what we can locate. It might take a while."

"That's fine. It should be something, I don't know...cozy?"

"Cozy." Dylan gave him a wide grin. "You bet. Elbow grease required, got it?"

"Yep. You know I can wield a hammer with the best of them."

Close to midnight, Marco finally headed to the bedroom they all shared. A group of twin beds were set up for those downtimes. It was like rooming with a bunch of brothers only one of whom was his actual brother. Said brother was already sleeping, snoring like a train. Nice.

Marco slipped in his wireless earbuds and started his playlist of rushing river sounds. The station happened to be the only place he had trouble sleeping. Speaking of trouble sleeping, his thoughts ran to Phoebe. She hadn't texted him once during his entire shift. He felt like a kid all over again, that heady rush of desire, adrenaline, and anticipation rendering him stupid with lust.

The sunset kiss shouldn't have meant anything at their age. They'd been too young. But if there was something to the legend, what would have happened if they'd never seen each other again? Other than Phoebe's wedding escape, and him wandering down the street minding his own business when her bag fell on his head, he might have never met her.

Strangely, the thought terrified him.

THE NEXT MORNING, after the exchange of information with the next shift, Marco left the station expecting to find Phoebe waiting in his truck. He found his truck, parked, with no one inside. He walked slowly to it, finding it unlocked, a note from Phoebe on the dashboard. She'd gone to get her car. Why *now*?

Even if she'd written she'd be back, what were the odds she could be talked into staying? After all, it could have been as simple as visiting for a few days while he was gone anyway. Marco wanted father and daughter reconciling. He believed this a great idea but wasn't certain Phoebe was strong enough yet to stand her ground. Her father, while a nice guy, would be versed at manipulation of his only daughter and after all, this was about family.

Those people who knew you best and exactly what lever to push. And while he thought Phoebe had grown a lot since her choice to abandon her former life, she hadn't had a whole lot of time. He would be lying to say he didn't understand the need to return to the safety of the only world she knew.

Telling himself not to panic, he found the keys in his glove compartment where she'd left them and drove like a mad man to the marina. If their adventure was over, he wanted to know and the sooner the better. Not finding any cars that didn't look like the usual suspects, he could feel his heart throbbing in his throat.

Gone. She was gone.

Back to the life she'd known where she probably had a lot

more room to stretch and grow. A second chance without the dead weight of an engagement she hadn't wanted. He ran down the pier to his boat slip, not bothering to wave hello to Drew or anyone else. If she'd left, he wanted to know. He'd then have to try to get back to some type of normalcy if he could.

Even if he was certain there would never be *normal* for him again.

But when he swung the door to his cabin open, Marco couldn't believe his eyes.

"Hi, Marco." Phoebe stood in the galley by the stove, stirring a pot. "I'm making you breakfast."

Her hair was tied up in a bun at the top of her head, small wisps of dark hair curling to the sides. Tendrils of steam rose from the pot, giving her cheeks a pink hue. Humming softly, she seemed like a fairy princess, and he half expected woodland creatures to pop out ready to render assistance.

He allowed himself a big intake of breath as the world righted itself.

"What's *wrong*?" She must have caught the stunned look in his eyes. "Rough shift?"

He hadn't fully expected to find her here and he wasn't quite sure what that said about him. Nothing good, he expected.

"Where's your car?"

"I had to park way down on the other side. Don't worry, it's a nice walk. I don't mind."

"It's not a nice walk if it's raining. You should have the closer parking space. C'mon, let's switch."

She wrinkled her nose. "As soon as this oatmeal is done. I'm not sure why cooking oats takes so long. I've been stirring for days. It has to be the perfect mixture of water and oats or it's too soupy or lumpy."

"You're making oatmeal for breakfast?"

She brightened. "With raisins, dates, and nuts. Healthy. It's going to be delicious."

He must look strange, standing like a statue that occasionally talked, watching her as though she was a particularly beautiful sunrise.

"Why are you giving me such a weird look?"

"I read your note."

"Well, I left it for you to read, silly."

"Yeah, but I guess I'm...surprised to find you here."

"Surprised? But I..." Her voice drifted off. "Oh."

"I'm sorry. But I didn't think—"

"Oh."

"Say something else, okay? You have to admit—"

"You didn't think I'd be back, did you?" She shut off the stove with a flick of her wrist and plunked both hands on her hips. "Wow. Just...wow. I thought *you* were different. I don't know what this says about all of you. Somehow the men in my life have no faith in me."

"No, I had faith. I...wait. The *men* in your life?"

"My father. *He* didn't think I'd manage without the credit card and expected that I'd be back. And as if that wasn't bad enough, you're the same."

"I'm sorry but it's your history. You get talked into things you don't want to do because you don't say 'no.' It's hard to know if anything you do is what you want, or if you're just going along with the flow."

"I've shown you that I've changed. Have I or have I not been disagreeable with you?" She came close, her dark eyes flashing with heat.

"You have."

This was something he'd never quite seen in her before. She was...angry. A righteous, burning frustration which was, let's face it, sexy as hell.

"Exactly. I asked for the better bed. I've told you to shut up at *least* once." She held up her fingers, counting off.

"True..." It was hard not to smile.

"Finally, I went to get my car, when *I* decided it was time. And came back because I wanted to."

All of this was true, but she shouldn't blame him for his doubts. He had almost nothing to offer her but himself. Maybe *he* wasn't enough. She was Silicon Valley royalty. How long could she be happy living a modest life? So far this was a grand adventure, but how long before he got on her nerves for working too hard? For being a stupid *guy*? Every abandonment fear he'd ever had rose to the surface. The panic he'd felt at thinking she'd left him could not be ignored. This had gone too far.

He'd lost his father, his hero, a larger-than-life presence in his family's home. Suddenly gone without any preparation. It caused a fissure in his world that he'd felt for decades. Maybe that had been the first time he realized even the people who love you leave. And from that moment on he'd relied only on his family and allowed women to breeze in and out of his life. With no commitments or expectations, saying goodbye was simple. Easy to move on.

"Look, Phoebe—"

"I have something to tell you." She held up a palm. "I accidentally overheard *Carrington Tech* is in trouble. More than anything, that's when I decided it was time to go see my father. *And* get my car."

"Okay."

She moved toward him, crossing the galley to his side. "We finally talked, *really* talked. And we're going to be okay. I found out he's lost his company. The company he built with my mother. They've been struggling for months and asked him to step down as CEO."

A sick feeling roiled in the pit of his stomach. "What does that mean, exactly?"

"*That's* the reason he wanted me to marry Ethan. I do feel better now that I know the truth. He thought I'd be 'taken care of.'" She held up air quotes. "Again, no faith that I could figure life out on my own. He thought that because of the way he'd raised me, I wouldn't know any other way to be."

"Isn't that…a valid concern?"

It might not be very enlightened of him, but he understood Mr. Carrington's worries. They were some of his own. Phoebe was new to being on her own and to relying only on herself. He didn't approve of Mr. Carrington's ways, but it made sense he wanted his daughter well provided for no matter what happened to him. Marco might have done the same. This was what love meant. Sacrifice. Doing what's best for someone else even if it's not your own desired outcome.

Phoebe stepped close, winding her arms around his neck. "I'm my mother's daughter. I can't seem to work up much interest in money other than how it can help others. And I sure don't care about clothes or shoes, at least not the way Flannery does. I don't need a fancy life. Money to eat and pay my bills is enough. And I know, that's a big deal here in the city."

It was, and she didn't know the half of it. She was still learning her way around her new independence. Still figuring out her life.

She cocked her head and took a step back. "What would you have done if I hadn't come back?"

"I'm mature enough to understand and respect your decision. You have to do what's best for you and your family."

"That's…very understanding of you."

Somehow, he got the distinct impression she wasn't happy with all of his mature understanding.

"I know family is important. To both of us." He took in a

deep breath. "And face it, our *families* are from two different worlds."

Strike two. Going by her frown she didn't appreciate this, either.

"That's not entirely true."

Marco had one last thing to reveal. He'd wanted to avoid this, but she had a right to know.

"Phoebe, I wasn't going to tell you this, but I think you should know. We've actually met before. Although like me, I'm sure you don't remember."

"When?"

"You and your mother were visiting my aunt at the boardinghouse. At the time it was our family home. My aunt had an art foundation and she worked with your mother. She must have invited her over."

"No wonder I thought the house seemed vaguely familiar, like somehow I'd been there before."

"That's not all. And I'm sorry to spring this on you, but when you hear, you'll probably think it's funny, too." He cleared his throat. "I kissed you at sunset. When I was five."

"*What?*" she gasped.

"Yeah, I know." He chuckled. "Apparently my cousin stole a toy away from you. I wrestled it back from him and gave it to you with a kiss."

"So, you…you kissed me…at sunset?"

"Yeah, but I feel like it must not count because we were so young."

This was his story, and he would stick to it. Even if meeting her was the closest thing to love at first sight, he would not tie her to him with a myth. Or a kiss at sunset, dawn, or noon. A lifetime of connection had to be more than this magnetic attraction. It had to be based on more than belief in a legend. There had to be a general cohesiveness, families who could blend well. As much as he liked Mr.

Carrington, he'd never fit in with his crowd, nor did he want to.

Bottom line, he and Phoebe were too different, sunset kiss or not.

"It counts. For me, it explains *everything*." She stared up at him with hooded eyes. "The reason I've felt this crazy way for you since the moment we met. You and I are fated."

That was the problem. He'd also seen the same damn shimmer. It meant they were each other's true loves. But only if he wanted to shackle Phoebe to him instead of letting her fly.

The overwhelming fear of loss loomed dark and ominous, pressing against him like a wall.

Black cloud, rolling in.

Some kind of realization seemed to cross her gaze. "Marco? Why didn't you tell me this sooner? Why were you keeping it from me?"

"I didn't want to hurt your feelings."

"You didn't want to hurt my feelings, or you were worried I'd insist you put a ring on it?" She held up her left hand.

"No. You don't understand."

He prepared to tell the biggest lie of his life to release them both from this unrelenting pressure brought about by a fantasy to control them both. One which he wanted nothing to do with. Because even if they were each other's true loves, she shouldn't be forever tied to him because of a kiss when they were just *children*.

"Phoebe, the truth is I don't think you and I are fated. I don't love you. And I'm sorry if that disappoints you."

MARCO WAS LYING.

Phoebe knew it with every rush of blood pumping

through her thudding heart. *Lying* to her face. He wouldn't even meet her eyes as he lied through his fool mouth. *Why?*

Was he really so fearful of commitment, stuck with being everyone's rebound guy, or was he simply afraid of a life with *her*? She realized she came with plenty of family dysfunction but someone who loved her was supposed to be able to look beyond all that baggage. She'd pressed forward, opening up her heart to a man who'd obviously never even considered settling down. Someone she'd been warned would *never* settle down.

Disappointment and pain clogged her throat, and she couldn't speak.

"Given more time, after all this adventure of yours is over, I think you might find I'm not the best man for you."

That royally pissed her off. The men in her life were always trying to decide *for* her. First her father, then Ethan. Apparently, Marco wasn't any different. She was so sick of it all, tired of fighting to be seen, to be heard, fighting so her own choices mattered.

"Why don't you let *me* decide what and who's best for me?"

"Look, we had a lot of fun and…and of course, I like the way we get along." He shrugged.

Good Lord, he sounded as though he were talking about the family pet. "Really? That's all you've got for me? We had *fun*? We get along?"

"I don't know what else you want me to say."

How about I adore you? You changed my life?

You're my soul mate. My true love.

All the things she could say about him.

"You love having sex with me, that much I do know. But apparently, that's all you love."

She'd made more out of their relationship because she'd experienced something she never had before with Marco.

But maybe he truly hadn't. Maybe he wasn't lying to her at all. Phoebe had made the mistake Veronica, and who knew how many before her, had made.

The assumption Marco could settle down for them. But he wasn't going to change. Not for his sunset kiss match, not for anyone. He liked his life exactly as it was, and she'd been another diversion for him.

Her sunset kiss match, the man she adored, didn't want anything to do with her and she'd now have to live with that for the rest of her life.

She almost wished she'd never met him or that someone else had been bumped over the head by her bag. Someone, who unlike Marco, would have kept walking.

Knowing what she had to do didn't make this any easier. Heartbeat pounding in her temples, she brushed by him.

"Where are you going?"

In the bedroom, she grabbed her bags and began shoving clothes inside. "I should go."

"You don't have to."

"But I can't stay. I love you with all my heart, Marco, and I probably always will." She heard the sound of her voice breaking. "That doesn't mean I have to be with you when you won't allow yourself to love me back."

A long beat followed, one which Phoebe hoped he'd fill. He didn't, at least not with the words she longed for.

"Where are you going? You don't have anywhere to go."

Marco had let her stay with him because he'd wanted to rescue her. There'd been no other option. The knowledge pierced her with a jagged edge. He couldn't turn her away because that wasn't in his nature. It was in his blood to rescue people. He was a hero through and through and she'd given him plenty of material.

Plenty to save.

"You don't have to worry about me anymore. Okay? I'm done being your problem. I release you from obligation."

"There's no obligation! I just want to know where you'll be and that you'll be okay."

"I will be." Phoebe straightened and walked right past him and up to the deck. "Trust me."

She took one last long look at the deck where she and Marco had watched dolphins swim and where they'd danced for the first time. These were the memories she'd made in a place where she'd fallen deeply in love. But funny, she didn't regret a thing. On this boat, she'd reclaimed her life. Now, it was time to go, and live the rest of it. However it might turn out.

"Phoebe, wait a second," Marco said as she easily bridged the gap between the boat and the pier without his assistance.

Her first time.

"Let's talk about this." He stood there, windswept hair giving him a roguish look. "Please don't go."

Thank goodness I had the presence of mind to get my car.

"Goodbye, Marco."

It's your Independence Day, Phoebe Carrington. Don't look back.

She walked as fast as she could to the other end of the pier, unclicked the lock on her sedan, and threw her duffel bags inside. She'd acquired a new bag since that first day Marco had taken her shopping, and both were stuffed with her secondhand finds. She hadn't even thought to bring her other clothes from home. It was a reflection of how little she cared about those designer labels, a closet filled with dresses that didn't mean a thing to her.

Phoebe pulled out of the marina parking lot without any idea where to go. She couldn't go home but she didn't have anywhere else to go. Her breaths were sharp and shallow in her chest.

If she went to Mrs. Reyes's boardinghouse, there would be far too many questions to answer.

By the time Phoebe arrived at her destination, tears slid down her cheeks. Hadn't she learned anything from all her failed relationships, or her wedding day fiasco? She'd gone from allowing her father control her to Ethan. And she'd nearly let Marco control her even if he hadn't tried. Her love had made her dependent on him just when she'd decided to start a new life. Her choices should have been different, but it seemed she wasn't ever able to simply choose herself.

Well, from now on she would.

She drove through the traffic of the morning and found a parking space a block away from Dawn's. Because it was a Sunday, Phoebe didn't know what to expect when she knocked. But she had to start somewhere. Above all, she wanted someone to talk to. A soft place to fall. She wished for the millionth time she could go home to her mother.

"Phoebe. What are you doing here?"

"I'm so sorry to bother you. Do you know of anyone looking for a roommate?"

"Come in," Dawn said.

Over tea and coffee, Phoebe told Dawn about leaving Ethan at the altar. Told him how condescending he'd been, how insufferable, how controlling. He wanted a woman he could mold into the perfect wife and he thought it had been Phoebe.

Then she explained how she'd met Marco, and the shimmering from the moment they touched. The new knowledge they'd actually first met and kissed as children but neither one remembered. The painful reality he was her true love, but it was entirely one-sided.

"Fascinating," Dawn said. "I've only heard about this kind of situation once before, but it makes sense. Of course, the sensations are more powerful when you meet your true love as a child. There's the purity of the heart which is especially open in children. No wonder your feelings were so powerful from the moment you reconnected as adults."

"Not that it makes a difference. He doesn't feel the same way about me. No shimmer."

Dawn patted Phoebe's hand. "I'm sorry, dear. This is a tough breakup for you. But, chin up! You'll find someone else. You're too young and pretty to give up on love."

"First, I have to be on my own for a while. I'm in no rush to get my heart broken again."

Of course, there was always the possibility that she'd never feel this way about anyone else. But she would not think about that now. Maybe, someday, she could find someone good enough. Or maybe, knowing what the real thing was like, she'd rather simply be alone. She could find companionship in friends. Coworkers. Family.

"Who knows? Maybe I'll be like your great-great-grandmother." Years apart with her true love, but eventually they'd be back together.

"I hope not. We turned that story around, but there's a tragic element in it, too. Some people wait around far too long for their soul mate." She took a deep breath. "As for your living situation, I have a duplex nearby. It's not cheap, of course, and I have a list of tenants fighting each other over the chance. The place is yours if you'll just do *one* thing for me. It could completely explode my business, or I wouldn't ask."

"Name it."

She leaned forward, a hint of mischief in her eyes. "Introduce me to Ethan Bellamy. If *I* can't find him the perfect bride, then it can't be done."

CHAPTER 17

"You call it madness; I call it love." ~ meme

Marco grew more disgusted with himself on a daily basis. After a week, he was still trying to go back to BP life, "before Phoebe." The pang and press in his chest had returned. But by now he recognized the difference between heartbreak and a heart condition. Good to know.

He'd finally let Phoebe go as he'd almost done the day at the bus stop. And he hadn't died. Unfortunately, he wasn't really living, either, mostly putting one foot in front of the other. It seemed he was happier before he'd ever been hit over the head by Phoebe Carrington, and he wished he could go back to the time before he'd ever met her. When he didn't realize what he'd been missing and before he knew how hard and fast his heart could open. But since returning to that moment couldn't happen without the benefit of a time machine (which he hoped Elon Musk would invent) *this* was his new reality.

He'd had something for a while, the kind of love sappy love songs and poems were written about. The type of connection most people search for, hope for, and dream about. And he'd walked away.

Fortunately, Dylan didn't ask questions. His big brother was a bit of a saint that way. Letting brothers come to him if they needed help, staying out of it when they didn't. He'd found a foreclosure two hours from the city and he and Marco would start rehabbing it once escrow completed. Marco would put in the sweat labor since Dylan had been the money man. They'd flip it, splitting the profits. A few more properties and Marco should have enough for a down payment on his own fixer-upper. Because it was time to move on from this nomadic existence. Not for Phoebe, or any other woman, but for himself. He was ready to take on more responsibilities, to grow and change. A house and a dog were good places to begin.

On Sunday morning, Marco had been sitting on the boat's deck, just staring out into the deep blue bay when Joe showed up unannounced.

"What are *you* doing here?" Marco asked.

Joe braced his long leg on the edge of the boat. "Want to go to Charley's?"

Because Marco didn't have anything better to do, they headed over to indulge in the neighborhood's favorite pastime of getting an extra donut just because it was so-called Miracle Sunday. Marco never realized how many traditions were built around the sunset kiss. Now there would be a sunset *stroll*, thanks to Phoebe's new employer. But hell, donuts were harmless enough. His major focus had been the Sunset Kiss Day event and sailboats, or, rather, how he could stay away from the tourist trap. Little did he know he'd already been sunk decades ago, before he even stood a chance.

He supposed now he would have to go through the rest of his life with this heaviness in his heart. Either that or ask Phoebe to live her life with a firefighter who attracted chaos. Invite her to be with a man who didn't know whether he *could* do commitment, even with his true love.

Face it, he'd have to drag her into life with a coward when it came to love. She deserved better. And what did he deserve?

He hated the words that immediately sprang: *a life without fear of abandonment.*

Because he'd survived a parent dying, but somehow, if he let himself fully love Phoebe and she left him, without a doubt he wouldn't make it through. Better to finish this before it even got started. If that sounded unheroic, well, he'd never claimed to be a hero. He just did his job and tried to help when and where he could.

"Ah, young Joseph and Marco!" Father Suarez turned, holding his pink box. "How is your daily good deed?"

"Nothing new," Marco said.

"Keep your eyes open. There are always possibilities." He shuffled off to find a seat.

After the Phoebe disaster, Marco thought maybe he should stay away from good deeds for a while. But only yesterday, he'd been minding his own business, and wound up helping a woman who'd locked her keys in the car with her two toddlers inside. She'd been in complete panic mode until Marco took over. It had seemed another silver-lining moment then, a time when he was able to help. But the good deed wasn't big enough. As someone who had thumbed his nose at true love, he figured he'd be atoning the rest of his life.

"Hey, guys!" Milly, Charley's sister, waved from a table where she sat with her husband and baby Coral. "Good to see you again."

The baby was cute, now over a year old if Marco had the age right. Milly and her husband were perfectly happy, and to his knowledge, no sunset kiss had ever been involved. Just failed birth control and two loving parents who were making it work.

"So, I'm thinking about moving back to the city," Joe said, once they'd grabbed a table.

"No kidding."

"I've been away long enough. Abuelita is getting older. It's time to come back, and it will be easier to help you and Dylan if I'm closer."

"What about the surfing business?"

"I can do that from anywhere at this point. It's almost on autopilot. I'll have to commute to Santa Cruz one day a week, maybe. It will work out." He cleared his throat. "And also…and I know this is crazy, so don't make fun. Okay?"

"You have my full attention."

"Well, that *is* impressive because the most beautiful woman I've ever seen just walked in the door." Joe stared over Marco's shoulder.

Marco didn't even turn around but took another bite of his muffin. "Are you going to tell me your crazy-pants idea, or what?"

"Wow." Joe gaped. "You didn't even *look*."

"No big deal." Marco shrugged. "I'm not interested."

"Why?"

"Maybe I'm thinking about being more than a rebound guy. More than Mr. Casual."

"I'm glad you said that bro. Because since you seem free and clear, you should go with me to the Sunset Stroll next week."

"Oh, Jesus."

"You'll like it. Very low-key, no kiss involved. You're matched up with a few prospects, have a drink, chat, end with a stroll outside. Then only the two of you decide if you'd like to see each other again. No pressure."

Marco appreciated no pressure, but he wasn't ready to even look at another woman.

"Phoebe works for the woman running it."

"Oh, yeah? Maybe I'll see her there. Should I say hi for you?"

"Don't bother. I can say hi for myself. And why are *you* doing a matchmaking event?"

"I like the idea of going a little deeper than a swipe across someone's photo. Too impersonal."

"I'm not interested. Let's see how it works out for you first."

"You're going to let *me* be the guinea pig?"

"Yeah," Marco said, sliding his brother a smirk. "You have to be good for something."

MARCO HAD BEGUN to think that his mother's sink was only plugged when she wanted to see one of her sons. But when he showed up to a foot of water in the kitchen, he knew his mother would not have purposely coordinated this.

How about that, a disaster not brought about by his mere presence. Okay, so maybe he'd let the black cloud status rule him. He was beginning to believe maybe it wasn't that *he* brought on the chaos, but he somehow managed to be where and when people needed help.

Probably not such a bad thing.

"This is going to take me all night," Marco complained. "Get Tutti to help mop all this water up."

"He's performing at the nightclub downtown. Marilyn Monroe night."

"Yay," Marco muttered.

"I'll help you, honey," his mother said, going at the mess with a kitchen towel.

At this rate, they'd be here all night. "You're basically putting a Band-Aid on a deep puncture wound."

"Mijo," Abuelita called out.

"No! Do *not* come in here." Marco held up his palm.

All he needed was his octogenarian grandmother slipping on the kitchen floor. He could handle only one epic disaster at a time, thank you very much.

"What did you do, Alice?" Abuelita went hands on bony hips. "How did you plug the sink this time?"

They went back and forth on how this could have happened and who put what down the garbage disposal until Marco wanted to stick pins in his eye sockets.

"I have a wet vacuum on the boat, maybe I should go get that."

Two minutes later, his mother came back with an old and dusty wet vac. "Will this work?"

Dad's old shop vac. A bit like falling into the past, and diving into an old and faded photograph. He hadn't seen this vacuum in decades and the pain that sliced through him was sharp and real and raw.

Ignoring the ache, he went to work, getting up enough water so that he could work under the sink for a while and find the issue. While under the dank and dark sink, a memory slipped back of hours spent with his father in his workshop. In that quiet place Marco and Dylan first learned how to work with wood, a skill they used to this day. His father gave that to his sons, including handing down a legacy of hard work and loyalty to a cause. To something greater than himself. Marco's issue wasn't actually with *commitment.* He was bound to the men he worked with every day, his brothers-in-arms. He was loyal. No, that was not the problem and it never had been. Deep down he'd always known this.

His problem was with romantic love. He'd been afraid that it would define him and turn him into someone he didn't want to be. But even though he'd changed, it turned out different didn't mean *less*. Still, growing up in Miracle Bay, he'd been indoctrinated into a belief that true love was the answer to the world's problems. But of course, it wasn't.

Wars still raged and people were killed every day trying to do the right thing.

Quite possibly he was overthinking this.

But damn it all, this was serious business, this love thing.

Mom walked back into the kitchen. "Well, I've got your grandmother settled for tonight."

"I think she might be losing her eyesight." Marco held up the corn husk he'd pulled out of the pipe. "She knows better."

"Oh, dear. She's definitely been distracted lately. Wondering when you and Joe will ever get married."

"Tell her to stop worrying about me."

"Really? And where is Phoebe tonight, the darling girl?"

"I have no idea."

"Oh, no. I really liked her and you're already moving on? It hasn't even been a month!"

Good to know his mother tracked the length of his relationships. She was dead-on. But a month or two went by effortlessly when spending time with someone who wasn't on his mind 24/7. With someone who didn't tie him up in knots.

But without Phoebe he felt like a leather jacket that had been left out in the sun for too long. Cracked, tough, ripped, and...broken.

"Everything was *different* with her."

"Yes, I noticed. Did you feel anything special when you kissed her?"

"Does it matter?"

"What kind of a question is that? Yes, it matters!"

"Yes, okay! Are you happy? I saw the stupid shimmer and glow! All over the damn place. I thought I might be having a stroke, but no, it's true love. Is that what it feels like to love someone? Because I'm not sure I want it. She makes me feel weak and needy."

"Do you really think falling in love makes a man *weak*?"

"Want to know what I think? I think Phoebe and I are a *disaster* on paper. No dating service would ever match us. We come from completely different backgrounds."

"It may seem that way but there are similarities in your families. Your values. We both know that Mr. Carrington is not a ruthless CEO. He cares about his community. And we all know about her wonderful mother."

"It goes beyond family. Even though Phoebe lost her mother, she's cheerful and optimistic. She believes in love at first sight. And I'm…shut down." He threw the wrench on the ground.

"I'm glad you finally admit it. That's why I hate those compatibility questionnaires. You can find out each other's favorite color and movie, but no one can tell when a heart will open wide enough to let love breeze right inside. Only the sunset kiss can do that."

So, they were back to this again. "Is that all you ever think about?"

"Open hearts? Yes. Without an open heart you can't experience the best from life. Both the highs and the lows. You can't experience real love without opening your heart. I would have spent a lifetime loving your father, but I only had twelve years. Still, I wouldn't trade them for anything in the world. Every day you're given with your true love is a gift. I wouldn't trade fifty years with the *wrong* man for one year with the right one. Yes, my heart was broken, but look at all

I've been given. Sons. A beautiful family. Good health. I'm still happy, and I want you to be happy, too."

His mother was close to tears. Dragging a hand down his face, he shut his eyes. He walked to her, taking her into his embrace.

"Okay. Don't cry. I'll think about what you said. I swear."

"Thank you." she sniffled. "Marco?"

"Yeah, what now?"

"Honey, you're filthy." She pulled back, plugging her nose. "And you stink, too."

He stood in his family's kitchen and laughed out loud for the first time in a week.

IF THE SUNSET Stroll wasn't a resounding success, it wouldn't be due to Phoebe's lack of effort. She'd done everything in her power to make the event a new Miracle Bay tradition. She'd written press releases, created a media kit, and slapped posters all over town:

COME to the first annual Summer Solstice Sunset Stroll where you just might meet your perfect match!

Speak to our matchmakers, have a glass of wine on us, and take a stroll together along the city streets.

If Dawn and Amanda can't find your perfect match, it simply can't be done!

Phoebe had created the ad copy and borrowed from Dawn's own words when she'd announced that if she couldn't find Ethan the perfect bride then it was impossible.

Between settling in to her side of the Victorian duplex she'd rented, and crying herself to sleep every night, she'd been slightly less than hopeful. Not just for herself, but for the human condition. If two people who fit together like she and Marco did couldn't wind up together, she didn't have a whole lot of hope for humanity. Yes, maybe she was prone to hyperbole, but she couldn't help herself.

Maybe she should start a support group for sunset kiss fails. Right now, she'd go to the meeting faithfully and bring the punch and cookies, too.

Today, two days before the big event, she would introduce Ethan Bellamy to Dawn. Just for fun, she'd chosen the Sunrise Bistro, not just to give Charley the business but because she hoped to somehow accidentally on purpose catch a Marco sighting. She arrived early to set the stage. Dawn wanted everything to be perfect for her appointment with Ethan. After introductions, Phoebe would ease out of the conversation.

Charley was her usual upbeat self, her cheeks pink with love.

"What are you doing this weekend?" Charley asked, as she led her to a cloth-covered table she'd set aside for the meeting with Dawn and Ethan.

"I'll be working the event."

"Dylan and I are taking Marco's boat and anchoring out for the entire weekend. I can't wait."

Just the sound of his name made an ache wind around Phoebe's heart and squeeze. Gosh, she missed the big lug. Missed his warm smile and chocolate-brown eyes. Missed the way he held her, making her feel precious and rare.

"It's nice of him to do that for you."

"He's moving, you know. Suddenly, life on a boat isn't what he wants anymore. He's looking for a house."

So, Marco was giving up his bachelor pad on water, his "tent with walls." It had been a cozy love nest to her. She had beautiful memories of that boat and hated that he might be trying to erase the time they'd spent together. But then again, this might not be about her at all. He was simply moving on.

"I always figured the yacht was a temporary stopgap for him. I feel bad because he gave up the house he and Dylan lived in so we could have our privacy."

"That was very nice of him."

"I was sorry to hear about you two. Please don't give up on him. If he's your soul mate, your true love, it will work out. Just look at me and Dylan. It took years."

"How's Marco doing?"

She always pictured Marco with his classically windblown hair, ruddy cheeks, devilish smile. At the time, she'd been on an adventure, but never dreamed she'd also fall in love.

"He's…intense. A little broody. Usually, Marco is so easygoing and carefree. Nothing rattles him."

"When you see him, tell him I said hello."

Dawn arrived on time, still cheery that Phoebe managed to schedule an introduction to Ethan. It had taken a dozen calls and eventually sending a bouquet of roses to his assistant, just so she'd put Phoebe's call through. But Phoebe would have given Dawn her firstborn for a chance to live in the duplex where Amanda lived on the other side. Okay, she was kidding. Mostly.

"Amanda is interviewing some of the matches we have in mind for Ethan today. We've extensively profiled him and know exactly who we're dealing with. So much to do, so little time! And our event is going off without a hitch thanks to you. I don't know what I ever did without you!" Dawn bubbled over with excitement. "Someday, you and I should talk about you opening up your own franchise of the Happy Matchmaker. You have the right heart for this type of business."

"Even if my own sunset kiss didn't work out?"

"Never say never." Dawn shook a finger. "You won't find

anyone who believes in love more than I do. I will *not* give up on you two."

Outside the glass picture window, Phoebe noticed as the sleek black sedan pulled up, stopped, and Ivan made his way to open the back-passenger door. "Here he is."

Ivan led the way, opening doors for Ethan, who couldn't be bothered to do it for himself.

"Are you sure you want to be blamed for fixing him up with someone?" Phoebe leaned in and whispered. "She might never forgive you."

"The challenge of a lifetime."

Introductions were made and Phoebe skillfully excused herself. Outside, the bright June day spilled over in spools of sunshine. She found Ivan leaning against the car, smirking, arms crossed.

"And I don't want to hear any lip from you!" Phoebe put up a hand.

"Good to see you, Phoebe. You should be congratulated."

This surprised her. "Who? Me?"

"They should erect a statue. Or at least name an app after you."

"I don't think this is funny."

"You said 'no' to Ethan Bellamy and no one says no to him."

Oh, right. She had done that. A slice of pride thrummed through her. "You should try it sometime. It's good for the soul."

"And the dude you ran off with? He pissed me off, too, but he has my respect. Ethan offered him money to tell us where you were, and he wouldn't do it."

This shouldn't have surprised Phoebe. She nodded, the knowledge a sweet ache.

"No, he can't be bought."

"She helped me. We helped each other. But it wasn't always easy, Pumpkin."

The words her father said about Mom, the love of his life, came back.

"I'll be ready for some tough times to come. And I won't give up."

It was what she'd told her father she would do. But how could she fight for someone who wouldn't even open up his heart to her?

She kept strolling down the street, feeling at home in her new city. Rejuvenated. She would make her own way, all part of her original plan.

Her duplex wasn't far from the bakery, a short walk. And then, speak of the devil, Phoebe saw Marco walking just ahead, one brother on each side. A dull and now familiar pain made its way from her heart to her stomach. He walked straight, and carefree, hands stuck in the pockets of his jacket, his head down.

On his way somewhere with purpose and intent. Not a care in the world.

By all appearances, he'd moved on.

CHAPTER 18

"I have found the one whom my soul loves." ~
Song of Solomon 3-4

As Marco approached Juan's Bar and Grill, he spied one of the flyers for the Sunset Stroll event. Lots of pink and red hearts. A sunset image at the top of the page, a shock to no one. Phoebe's event. A couple of days ago, he'd been walking toward Charley's shop and caught Phoebe sticking up the poster on the plate glass window.

He'd turned and walked the other way before she saw him. It stung to see she'd moved on so easily without breaking her stride. *Love, love, love.* Maybe she'd find her dream of forever with this matchmaking event. Screw it all. He didn't care anymore.

Last night, he'd laid down on his bed, taking up all the space. He thought he'd miss that when he started sleeping with Phoebe. It was the other way around. There was too much damn space now.

His foul mood continued as he racked up points at the pool table. The lousy attitude deepened when the waitress got his order wrong. It took a massive hit when someone recited stats on the Niners' chances at the next Super Bowl. And then some guy came in and announced how he'd signed up for the Sunset Stroll and met a beautiful girl named Phoebe.

"I want to see if we can be a match," the dude said. "She's going to be there anyway and she's free and single."

Marco wished he could hit something. "Is that what she told you?"

"Yeah. The matchmaker said some bozo broke her heart and she knows pretty soon she'll be open to a match again. Why?"

Mine! We kissed at sunset!

Shit! What the hell had gotten into him?

Joe winced. Dylan closed his eyes and pinched the bridge of his nose.

"No reason," Marco spit out. "Rack 'em up, Joe. I'll beat your skinny ass all over again."

But even another win didn't cure his attitude.

"It's time for me to go home," Marco said, shrugging into his jacket. "I'm not fit for company."

"You're right about that," Dylan said. "But you're sticking around so we three can have a chat."

They headed to a booth where Marco would probably get chewed out for being the Debbie Downer of the evening. No one expected *anger* from Marco Reyes, just fun and carefree times. Maybe he was tired. Considering his entire world had been turned upside down, no wonder.

Joe hooked a thumb in Dylan's direction. "Remember last year when you and I had to rescue Dylan from making the biggest mistake of his life by letting Charley go to Paris?"

"As I remember, he moped around for a while." Marco elbowed Dylan.

"I thought if Charley stayed with me instead of taking that chef job, she'd always regret it. But as you two pointed out, *she* didn't want to go. She made the choice to stay, and it wasn't for me to tell her that she hadn't made the right one." He leaned back, smug. "As it worked out, of course she made the right choice. And so did I."

"But that's my problem," Marco said. "Phoebe can do better than me. And we're from such different worlds."

"She's different than I expected given how she was raised. And you fit together," Joe said. "It's obvious to everyone."

Dylan took a pull of his beer and set it down. "What you're missing is that she wants to be part of our world. I see she didn't go back home to her father or her ex-fiancé. She wants a different life and she's making it for herself. You got to admire that."

"It's also the pressure of all this sunset kiss stuff. We kissed as kids, lived in different worlds, and still we ran into each other again. It's like something out of a movie. Fate. And I guess I'm afraid if I ruin this, I'm done for."

"Well, you might be done for either way," Dylan said.

"It all happened so fast," Marco thought, and then realized he'd said those words out loud. "I guess I wasn't ready for her."

"Look," Joe said. "I've known for a long time that I have to work twice as hard as anyone else in the room. It's made me deadly persistent and a sharp businessman. But everything has always come easily to you. Just kind of dropped in your lap. You haven't had to work too hard for anything in your life. You sailed through school with top grades. You were hired through an open call. I'm sure passing the LT test is going to be a breeze. Work. Women. It all just came to you.

Even Phoebe! She literally fell into your life. This isn't even a *metaphor."*

Was that true? Marco had never spun it that way. He was the easygoing brother, sandwiched between serious Dylan and wild Joe. Nothing he'd ever attempted to do had been too hard for him, and maybe in some ways he'd become lazy because of it. Every time he had to make an effort, work for something, mostly relationships, he tended to bail.

It was a tough truth to admit.

"You know that feeling you have in the pit of your stomach right now? The tightness in your chest? Get used to it, because that's never going to go away until you fix this." Dylan poked Marco's chest. "And how's that any better?"

Marco scowled. "Are you going to sit here and tell me because I'm already miserable I might as well go all in?"

"What I'm saying is it sounds like she's worth going all in. With whatever it is: true love or not. You gotta give it a chance. Unless, of course, you want *that guy* to waltz right in on Sunset Stroll day." Dylan pointed to the guy who'd come in and announced to everyone that he hoped to be matched with Phoebe.

"Yeah, he's not her type," Marco said.

"No, *you* are."

Marco shook his head, a rare and piercing understanding hitting him. If he wanted Phoebe, he would have to admit the truth. He'd been struck dumb and stunned from the start. He loved her. If she wanted to be stuck with him...well, he wanted to be "stuck" with her.

Forever.

"Damn, I'm an idiot."

Not all that long ago, he'd told Dylan that if a woman ever looked at Marco the way Charley did Dylan, he might consider a commitment. Because women loved Marco, but they were attracted to the wrong things about him. They wanted a good time, they wanted casual, and somewhere along the line Marco had settled for this, too.

And easy got him pretty far in life until the road ended right at Phoebe Carrington's feet.

Marco pulled into the parking lot of Chef Chu's restaurant and strolled toward the entrance. Today, he had an appointment with destiny. Or at least, that's what his mother would call this moment. Maybe even his father, who had believed in love as much as his mother did. Though Marco still missed him, every day, he now believed he'd be proud of the man Marco intended to be from this point forward. He'd approve of his plan.

Today, he had a meeting with the man who could make the ultimate difference for the rest of Marco's life. This man would either make or break his future, because the future couldn't get started without him.

But of all the pictures of David Carrington swimming around in Marco's head, he didn't meet any of them. Marco had done his due diligence and scoured photos on the web. In those, Mr. Carrington had always been dressed in a suit, looking like the classic CEO.

The hostess guided him to the table where Mr. Carrington sat, perusing the menu. A cross between a geek and an aging frat boy, he wasn't wearing a black turtleneck, but a flannel shirt. Meanwhile, Marco had dressed in the best shirt he owned, a blue button-down with a matching tie.

"Good to meet you." Mr. Carrington put down his menu and shook Marco's hand. "Have a seat. Now, what can I do for you? You said you graduated from a San Francisco school I supported with donations."

Ah, yes. This meeting had been arranged when Marco, as a graduate of a school Mr. Carrington had funded in the past, wanted to speak to the CEO about the tech industry. And like so much in his life, the appointment came easily to Marco. The rest of this conversation, however, might be the toughest one he'd ever had.

"First, let me just thank you for all your support of the public schools in my area. And for sending so many under-privileged kids in my area to college."

"It's my pleasure. My wife, Becky, and I always believed in paying it forward."

"Second, I'm not here to talk about technology."

"No?"

"This is about Phoebe."

Mr. Carrington quirked a brow. "And how do *you* know my daughter?"

Marco cleared his throat. "That's a long story. Basically, I cushioned her fall from a fire escape."

"Jesus." Mr. Carrington's face went pale.

"Yeah, well, you know your daughter better than I do. She wanted to get away from her wedding and it was an old fire escape, not entirely her fault."

"You were the person who helped Phoebe get away? Who gave her shelter?"

Marco winced. "Yes, sir. Let me explain—"

Mr. Carrington reached across the table and offered his hand. "Thank you."

Relief flooded through Marco, but if he was any kind of father, Marco hoped Mr. Carrington would understand and be grateful.

"At first, I didn't know who she was. But I had to honor her wishes. She didn't want to go home though she knew she'd have to fix things with you. I'm glad she did."

"You're the firefighter. She told me about you."

"I figured she might. We spent time together, I got to

know your daughter, and how special she is. We fell in love. I…I fell in love with her."

"I gathered that." Mr. Carrington's lips were tight.

"So, here's the thing. I'm studying for the lieutenant exam and I know I'll pass it on my first try. Studying and school has always come easily me. In fact, this is the hardest thing I've ever done." Marco tugged on the tie he wasn't accustomed to wearing. Jesus, he was probably blowing this. "You might not think I'm right for Phoebe, but I promise I'll love her and take care of her for the rest of my life. If she'll have me."

Mr. Carrington lips went from a straight line to quirking in amusement. Maybe he enjoyed watching Marco squirm.

"If you know my daughter, as you say you do, you obviously know you won't be able to take care of her. She will resist that, much as she might occasionally need some guidance at the very least. Such as, when climbing down a fire escape." He dragged a hand down his face. "But don't make the same mistake I did, doubting that she knows what's best for her. She has her own mind, just like her mother did."

"I have to agree with the own mind part."

Mr. Carrington chuckled. "Son, I've enjoyed this. You're not the first man who's ever had to sweat in front of a woman's father. I appreciate the fact you were willing to do so, even though you don't have to. Her approval is all you really need."

"Maybe so, but family means a lot to me, too, and I would appreciate your…um, blessing." With that he tugged on the damn tie again, closer to his neck this time.

He felt a bit as if he'd stepped into the previous century and only wished Abuelita could see him now. She'd no doubt be impressed.

"Family meant a lot to Phoebe's mother, too. She was the heartbeat of ours, and unfortunately when I lost her, I let everything go. All the sense of community and family she created, all gone with her. I can now see how much Phoebe missed it."

"I hope she and I can create our own family. One day."

Mr. Carrington blinked. "I'm impressed. This *is* serious."

"I'm talking about forever." Marco cleared his throat. "Sir."

Mr. Carrington leaned back in his seat. "Call me David."

ON THE DAY of the Sunset Stroll, the cafe was filled with men and women yearning to find "the one," and the turnout for their first annual event was better than anyone had expected. Within an hour of their start, the sun's rays would slowly dim, the softness of the long summer day coming to an end.

Two weeks after she'd last seen or talked to Marco, Phoebe was still regaining her footing. She told herself that maybe she and Marco might simply need a little time apart. A breather. They'd met suddenly and fallen so quickly she understood why he'd be leery, and why he might want to take a step back. She didn't exactly come with the best endorsement for past relationships, having left one groom at the altar.

But she'd discovered something interesting about herself. She didn't want a relationship for the sake of being part of a couple. She'd been hit on repeatedly in the last week, once by a man who'd shamelessly flirted with her when he signed up for the Sunset Stroll. Handsome though he was, he didn't do a thing for her. Not like Marco, who made it hard for her to breathe when he simply smiled.

"They're all going to *eat*, right?" Charley waltzed out from the kitchen.

Phoebe had tried to get Charley to kick back and let them take over all the organizing, but when it came to food,

Charley couldn't be restrained. The event had turned from cocktail hour to appetizers.

"Oh yes, of course."

"Because what someone eats says a lot about who they are."

"I'll make a note," Phoebe said, then scratched her temple. "You know, Marco made me a PLT not long ago. Pancetta, lettuce, and tomato."

Charley nodded, adjusting her chef's hat. "Yes, of course he did."

"Um, care to translate?"

"Marco is both unique and sexy, like pancetta instead of plain bacon. And he's also down to earth: lettuce and tomato."

"Oh, I see."

"You know, I can make almost any entrée in existence and do it quite well. French, Italian, Continental, Chinese, you name it. But when I ask Dylan what dish he'd like me to cook for his birthday, anything at all, he always wants my homemade mac and cheese."

"What does that tell you about him?"

Charley winked. "I'll never tell."

Minutes before they were to start, Amanda took both Dawn and Phoebe aside. "There's a guy out here who didn't sign up and wants to drop in."

"Do we have room?" Dawn flipped through her list.

"Yes, but he hasn't even filled out the questionnaire. He says he doesn't believe in that sort of thing. Says he'll 'know when he sees her.'" Amanda held up air quotes. "To be honest, at least six of our women already want to take a stroll with him."

A stroll. Had they simply created a new euphemism for hooking up?

"I don't like the idea," Phoebe protested. "We can't let this be a casual place to pick someone up. Our candidates should be serious. Ready for commitment to one person. He should fill out the questionnaire and come back another time."

"I agree but he does have an honest look about him. For what it's worth, I don't think he's on the make."

"Amanda does have a good sense about this. We better make room," Dawn said. "Can't ever have enough happy couples matched. What's the man's name?"

"Marco Reyes," Amanda said, and Dawn added him to the list.

Oh. God. Phoebe took in a shaky breath.

So, Marco had come to *her* event to pick someone up and Phoebe was to sit by and watch this happen. Her stomach twisted and roiled. Surely, she should not have to witness this fiasco unfold.

"I don't feel well. I think...I might have a fever." Phoebe lowered her hand to her belly.

She'd used the same childhood excuse when she desperately wanted to get out of an awkward social situation. When she didn't want to attend a classmate's party and be the only one who didn't know how to talk to people. When she didn't want to go to gym class and be the last one picked for the team sport.

"Oh dear." Dawn reached out with the back of her hand and touched Phoebe's forehead in a motherly way. "Better go home and straight to bed with you. Don't worry about a thing."

"Yeah, hon," Amanda said. "You've done enough. We've got this."

Oh whew. They had this. They had *her*. It felt like the old days when her mother covered for her, when she eased the way forward for Phoebe. Yes, she'd depended on her mother far too much and it had been Phoebe's downfall when no one else understood her. Even her own father. But she'd come a long way recently and knew she'd be okay. She would no longer avoid most uncomfortable situations. She would, however, guard her heart. Supremely. No one, least of all Dawn and Amanda, could blame her.

Hurrying out the back door of the Sunrise Bistro, and waving to Charley with a quick excuse, she arrived home within minutes. Opening the door, she felt the comfort and relief of her own little slice of the city. Home. No matter how far out of her comfort zone she grew, Phoebe would always prefer the quiet times. And she'd designed her duplex to be a soft place to fall. Slowly, she'd furnished the place with garage sale finds and decorated with pops of color. In the center of the living room sat a green secondhand love seat filled with blue, orange, red, and yellow pillows. Framed photos of sailboats hung on her walls, along with pictures of old trolley cars and the San Francisco skyline. A few photos of Phoebe and her parents in earlier years. One of her and Aunt Sarah at her college graduation.

Absolutely no framed sunsets, thank you very much.

She'd been a small child when she met the love of her life and, hence, had no way of knowing how her future would unfold without him. But it warmed her heart to know her mother had met Marco at least once. She'd seen the boy who would become the man Phoebe would someday fall in love with. Maybe not the man she'd wind up with, but the man she'd fortunately, or unfortunately, always love him. And the knowledge she had this small connection with her mother even after all these years felt significant. Important.

What if she'd gone through with the wedding to Ethan? Would she have gone her entire life never again meeting Marco Reyes? As a true romantic, it wasn't difficult for Phoebe to believe in destiny. If she and Marco were fated, they'd have found a way to be together. Someday. Even if she was eighty, and a widow given a second chance to love.

No matter how much she hurt right now, she couldn't regret meeting him. She wasn't sorry she'd fallen in love.

But she wasn't going to watch him find someone else at her matchmaking event.

Really, of all the nerve.

Phoebe changed into sweats and fuzzy slippers. She pulled out a tub of ice cream and got cozy on her couch, throwing a blanket over her legs. Next month, Flannery would visit for the first time. Her father said he'd come, too, as long as work didn't intervene. No shock, he was on to his next project, pulling in long hours according to Aunt Sarah. Already had a slew of new investors lined up.

A knock at her door surprised Phoebe because Amanda was the only one who occasionally popped over to check in. Phoebe peeked through the keyhole before unlocking any of the many locks on her front door.

Marco. It was Marco.

"Phoebe? Come on out," he called out. "I know you're in there."

"What are *you* doing here? Shouldn't you be at the event trying to score?" she said through the door. "Lots of women there, ripe for the picking."

"Open this door, please."

"No, I don't think so."

"C'mon, I need to talk to you. Hurry. It's important."

She took a smidge of pity on him when he sounded desperate, and unlocked all deadbolts, leaving only the flimsy chain anyone with a little muscle could knock down.

"What is it?"

"Will you come out here and talk to me?"

"It depends. Are you here to apologize for showing up at *my* event to hook up with someone else?"

"I can't apologize for that because that's not why I went. I came with Joe. And also, to make sure you didn't wind up with some dude named *Jared.* He has a thing for you."

Jared? Who in the world is Jared?

"Please come outside. We're running out of time."

At this odd statement, Phoebe unhooked the chain and opened the door wide. "What do you mean by that?"

He retreated to the sidewalk where the buildings didn't block the rays of fading sunlight.

"Come here. The sun is about to set."

Her pulse kicked up. "We…you and I don't have to…we already…"

"Please."

She stepped outside because maybe, just maybe he'd feel something this time. The hopeful side of her clung to the possibility. But this moment could either be the confirmation of her worst fears, or everything she'd ever wanted.

He took her hands and tugged her to him. "The first time we did this we were only children. See, that's the trouble with a kiss. Timing."

"It has to come when you're ready, and your heart is open."

"Unless it's always open. Like yours." He squeezed her hands.

He kissed her as the sun slid down in a soft haze. Everything around Phoebe shimmered and glowed and electricity pulsed between them, thick and unbreakable. She fisted his shirt, hanging on to this incredible sensation that left her feeling both raw and new. It seemed as if their kiss lasted a lifetime, comprised of every hope, yearning, and belief to create a lover's dream. A dream that prayed for a second chance.

When Marco broke the kiss, they were bathed by the ambient light of the streetlamp and faint moonglow.

His eyes crinkled in the start of a sly smile.

"Did you see anything…special?" Phoebe gnawed on her lower lip. "D-different?"

"You mean glowing and shimmering."

"Yes."

"Like the Fourth of July."

"Really? Oh, Marco!" She could hardly contain her excitement, going up on the balls of her feet to hug him tight.

"Just like the moment we met."

"Huh?"

"I didn't even want to admit it to myself. But I saw glowing and shimmering like an aura. I thought maybe I was having a stroke after you jumped me. But no, I was reuniting with my sunset kiss."

"You've felt this all along?"

"Phoebe, after you left, I thought I was dying. I was supposed to move on. But that didn't work, because I love you. I loved you the moment you literally fell into my life, and forgive me if I wasn't ready for you. For all of this. Things have always come easily to me. Even love. I know this doesn't happen every day. You only meet your true love once in a lifetime. *If* you're lucky. And what if I were to blow our only chance? *Your* only chance?"

"It figures you would think you're responsible for my happiness, too, but you don't have to rescue me. Not anymore."

"You rescued yourself."

"It doesn't mean I don't believe in heroes because I do. You're mine, whether you want to be or not. I knew I'd always love you, but I just wasn't sure we'd be able to be together."

"I want to be yours, Phoebe. More than anything." He pressed his forehead to hers. "I love you."

"Then we can't lose. We have it all! We're a sunset kiss match. And we have the triangle Dawn talks about: love, companionship, and magnetism. But we need one more thing."

"What's that?"

"To bring our families together. You need to talk to my father."

"Way ahead of you, babe." He swept her up in his arms and carried her back to the house. "Way ahead of you."

EPILOGUE

"If I loved you less, I might be able to talk about it more." Jane Austen (Emma)

Two years later

In the year and a half since Phoebe Carrington became a matchmaker, she'd personally witnessed two weddings come from her matches. She adored being a part of a couple's special day. Always invited. Always happy to celebrate love in all its many forms.

Today, the bridal bouquet was a beautiful mix of yellow daffodils and blue hydrangeas, resembling picked wildflowers. Perfect. The dress, too. Not a huge poufy monstrosity but a mermaid-style dress with a tight-fitting bodice, slight flare, and *short* train.

Phoebe took one last glance in the mirror and adjusted her veil. Everything was precisely as she'd wanted. No big gala but a simple church wedding with family and close friends followed by a reception at the Reyes family home. No tiara this time, but the old-school classic headpiece handed down by Mrs. Reyes. First to Charley, then to Phoebe.

The day had come for her wedding. Again.

This time she wouldn't run out even if the church itself went up in flames, a comical thought considering her groom.

For a while she worried the Catholic Church might spontaneously combust as Father Suarez had requested special dispensation to marry a Protestant at the main altar. But he insisted he couldn't have anyone else marry Marco.

Interestingly, she'd learned that at least part of Marco's reticence had been the sanctity with which he viewed marriage.

"I'm only doing this once, so be sure," Marco had said. "Because it won't be easy to get rid of me once we make those vows."

She was counting on it.

During their pre-marriage counseling sessions, Phoebe discovered that Marco had taken a challenge posed by Father Suarez. One good deed daily. He'd been blessed with good fortune and the uncanny ability to be exactly where he'd be needed. Pay it forward.

It was at least part of the reason he'd stopped to help her that fateful first day. His good deed.

The rest of it, if you were a believer, was their destiny. She and Marco were always intended to meet again someday, and they did indeed, in the most inopportune way.

Who else but a firefighter would *rescue* his fated mate?

Funny, but of all the things Phoebe Carrington imagined she'd do with her English degree, becoming a matchmaker had not even been on the radar. But when Amanda Sheridan opened her franchise of the Happy Matchmaker, she asked Phoebe to join her, declaring her a "natural." She didn't know whether or not that was true, but perhaps she had just been lucky on her first try.

Thanks to her, Joe Reyes was engaged to the woman Phoebe had introduced him to. With all the Reyes men either married or engaged, Alice and Abuelita threw a party for Phoebe, and declared her a "daughter" forever.

One could say that life was great all around.

Everyone was happy, even those who didn't necessarily deserve to be. Two months after Ethan Bellamy married a twenty-five-year-old former model Dawn had arranged for him to meet, Dawn collected a hefty fee and happily retired. She now lived on an island off the Pacific Northwest with her husband, where they collected rents and Happy Matchmaker franchise fees.

"Are you ready, Pumpkin?" her father asked, straightening his tie.

I was ready the day I met Marco she almost said out loud. Instead, she picked up her bouquet and accepted her father's arm.

"Let's do this."

At the entrance to the church doors, her father turned to Phoebe. "It's not too late to walk out."

"Daddy, please. That's not funny."

"I had to be sure." He patted her arm as his lips quirked in a smile.

"He's the one. I have zero doubts."

The music began to play, and everyone stood as she and her father made their way down the aisle. Amanda winked happily from next to her newly reconciled husband, the handsome Noah Sheridan. The church was filled with the large extended Reyes clan, and all of Phoebe's new friends from her work as a matchmaker. There were Gerianne and Henry, smiling back. They were new. So were Aunt Sarah and her beau, William, who might not have found each other without Phoebe's matchmaking skills. Last but not least, Daddy would be next. Oh yes, she'd find the right woman for him. Mom would have wanted it that way.

At the altar, the padre stood flanked by their small wedding party: Charley and Cousin Flannery on one side, Dylan and Joe on the other.

And stepping forward to meet her, smiling at her as though he'd seen her for the first time, Lieutenant Marco Reyes, the man who still made her heart stop every time she saw him. His hair was recently trimmed and styled neatly, and not as she preferred, on the wrong side of a cut. The way it had been on the day he'd proposed, the seagulls cawing, the waves crashing, his hair disheveled and windblown, cheeks ruddy. He'd dropped to one knee six months to the day after they met and thanked her for putting up with him. For the long hours he worked, for the other hours he spent studying for the exam, or rehabbing fixer-uppers.

Then he'd asked her if she'd mind very much putting up with him for the rest of her natural life.

"There's nothing I'd rather do," she'd said between tears as he slipped the ring on her finger.

Father Suarez cleared his throat, snapping her back to the present. "We are gathered here today to witness the marriage of Marco Antonio Reyes and Phoebe Rebecca Carrington."

ALL THE PEOPLE Marco loved were gathered in the very home where he'd met Phoebe Carrington for the first time.

The deep back patio of the boardinghouse turned out to be the perfect place for their reception. Fairy lights were strung from tree to tree, and outdoor tables set up under large parasols. Charley would hear of no one else catering the dinner though since she also served as a bridesmaid, she'd accepted Mr. Carrington's help to hire a staff. Still, she flitted around, checking the food to be sure it was served as she'd demanded, um, instructed.

In the very back of the patio and on a temporarily constructed stand were Tutti and members of his newly formed band.

Last week, Marco's mother had given them a wedding gift, a local artist's rendition of an old photo she'd found. It had been taken the night Becky Carrington had visited them so many years ago, little Phoebe sitting on her lap. Members of his family were in the photo, too, memorialized for posterity. His father's smiling face turned to the camera as he held little Joey in his arms. His mother's hands, one on Dylan's shoulder, and one on Marco's. A snapshot in time of two young children who'd had no idea that at least a part of their future was determined that same night.

"Ladies and gentlemen, our bride and groom will now join us for their first dance," Tutti announced.

"Can't Help Falling in Love" played through the outdoor speakers, Tutti's smooth velvety voice a dead ringer for the King's.

Marco took his bride's hand and led her to the center of the patio where he twirled her around to the *ooh*s and *aah*s of the crowd.

Some things are meant to be...

True enough, and Marco would no longer fight his destiny. Especially not when it entwined him with this woman, gorgeous both inside and out. A life with her at his side would be richer than he'd allowed himself to hope.

ALSO BY HEATHERLY BELL

LUCKY COWBOY

NASHVILLE COWBOY

BUILT LIKE A COWBOY

COWBOY, IT'S CHRISTMAS

WINNING MR. CHARMING

GRAND PRIZE COWBOY

THE ACCIDENTAL KISS

THE CHARMING CHECKLIST

Coming soon:

MR. COWBOY

For a complete book catalog, please visit the author's website.

ABOUT THE AUTHOR

Heatherly Bell is the author of over thirty-four published contemporary romances under two different pen names.

She lives for coffee, craves cupcakes, and occasionally wears real pants. She lives in Northern California with her family.

Made in the USA
Monee, IL
10 March 2022